THE WORK OF CHAD OLIVER

MORE WILDSIDE CLASSICS

Please see www.wildsidepress.com for a complete list!

THE WORK OF CHAD OLIVER

An Annotated Bibliography & Guide

by

HAL W. HALL

WILDSIDE PRESS

For Chad, of course

THE WORK OF CHAD OLIVER

This edition published in 2006 by Wildside Press, LLC.
www.wildsidepress.com

ISSN 0749-470X

BIBLIOGRAPHIES OF MODERN AUTHORS, NO. 12

THE WORK OF CHAD OLIVER
An Annotated Bibliography & Guide

by Hal W. Hall

CONTENTS

ACKNOWLEDGMENTS

The creation of a bibliography is rarely a task completed without the help of others. This volume owes much to a number of individuals. Special thanks go to Chad Oliver, who provided information, caught mistakes, edited the interview, and generously added a postscript to bring the interview up-to-date. Without Chad's help, the bibliography would have been incomplete.

Many others helped in providing information, or talent to make this volume possible. To each of you, a sincere "Thank you!":

Richard D. Boldt
Yvonne Knudson
Bill Page
Doug Potter
Cathy Rylander
George Slusser
Howard Waldrop

INTRODUCTION

Writing about Chad Oliver is a lot like writing about the voice out of the whirlwind.

Thirty years ago I read *Mists of Dawn*. I didn't know who Chad was and I didn't care. All I knew was that I wanted to go punch out Neanderthals and Cro-Magnons, and I went looking for them. It dampened my enthusiasm a little when I learned you had to have a time machine to do it. I'm sure my fascination with time travel and alternate worlds started then, and Chad is to blame.

The usual biography runs this way: Symmes Chadwick Oliver was born March 30, 1928 ("the year Margaret Mead published *Coming of Age in Samoa*") in one of those Ohio towns that starts with a C, that he caught rheumatic fever when he was fourteen, that the family moved to Crystal City, Texas, and (through football and other sports) Symmes C. Oliver, the 90-lb. weakling, became Chad, the Mountain Who Walks. (Chad is tall, muscular and devilishly handsome, but he says he "hates those biographical notes that make it look like I ride in on my Brahma bull, throw my hat on the antler rack and pound my typewriter with both fists.")

He studied both English and anthropology at UT (and wrote one of the first master's theses on science fiction, "They Builded A Tower"), then did his doctoral work in anthropology at UCLA. He returned to the University of Texas where he has been ever since (they've made him chairman of the Department of Anthropology three or four times). His specialties have been the Plains Indians and the Kamba of East Africa, with whom he spent a couple of years of field work. ("If my life would have been written by a sentimental SF writer, I would have been called B'wana Rocket.")

Chad's also written a few things. What I'd like to do is tell you about the devious path by which he came to write all the things in this bibliography. I don't think it's been told before.

Chad read when he was a kid, but he also fished, played football and baseball, the usual boy stuff. When he had the attack of rheumatic fever, he was forced to read a lot. What he was mainly reading was what we call Air War Fiction—*Dusty Ayres and his Battle Birds*, *G-8 and his Battle Aces*. He wrote fan letters to the magazines—the editor used to sign his letters back to Chad, "Clear skies and tailwinds," and was going to use Chad as one of G-8's battle chums or something, but the magazine folded and that's another story.

What happened was that one month along with the usual pulps, Chad's mother brought him a copy of a lurid magazine with the novella, "Treasure on Thunder Moon" by Edmond Hamilton, in it. When Chad finished it his immediate thoughts were: a) this is the greatest novel ever written, and b) is there more of this stuff out there?

Chad ran out of his house, jumped on his bike (illness be damned, this was literature!), hot-pedalled it to the nearest newsstand, and bought everthing that looked vaguely like the magazine he had just read.

And so it started. You can look through old *Startling* and *Thrilling Wonder Stories* and find letters signed "Chad Oliver, the Loony Lad of Ledgewood." Then Chad moved to Crystal City with his family and won friends and admirers (and gained pounds) through sports (even so, some of his teammates later told him that "the kind of guy who reads books we usually kill and throw in ditches").

Along about 1947 he and the one other guy in Texas (besides Tom Reamy) who read SF put out a fanzine called *The Moon Puddle*, and used such high-class pseudonyms as "L. Sprague de Willey."

Chad had read so much of the stuff that he had begun to write it, story after story, about a week after his fifteenth birthday. After six years of sending them off, one day the editor of *F&SF* wrote back: "We love your story, but we won't be able to publish it for some months. If you'd like it back to sell it to someone who'll publish it sooner, we'll understand." ("Hell," said Chad, "I would have paid Anthony Boucher to publish it!")

And then came all the stories, the novels *Shadows in the Sun*, *The Winds of Time*, *The Shores of Another Sea*, *Another Kind*, *The Edge of Forever*, his award-winning Western, *The Wolf is My Brother*, and his anthropology textbook, *The Discovery of Humanity: An Introduction to Anthropology*.

I'd like to say a couple of things about Chad Oliver the writer. Too many critical articles refer to him as an anthropological SF writer—many of his stories concern the relations of men and women, men and men, men and aliens, and the continuation of traditions, whether of the small tribe or the local star system.

To think of Chad this way is to miss about half the things he's written. Look at "Didn't He Ramble," his story about jazz music and what it's all about, probably the best SF ever written about that music.

Go find "Transformer," which is from the point of view of the little plastic people who live in an HO gauge model railroad town, which is owned by a mean kid who likes to crash trains together, or to run them so fast the flagman Humphrey has to run out of his little booth and signal like mad every 37 seconds. It's one of the finest and funniest fantasies ever written.

His stories "King of the Hill" and "Ghost Town" are about, not the survival of mankind, but of intelligence, two very different things. (Chad said in the Afterword to "King of the Hill" that "Man is the ape that walks like a chicken.")

The things Chad does away from the typewriter aren't the major concern of this bibliography, but I'll mention them anyway. Students pack his Intro to Anthro classes to hear the famous lecture in which he imitates, in order, all the warning calls of the higher primates. Chad loves to teach, and has gone to a lot of trouble to find the answer to a question he didn't know asked by a student who didn't care.

He used to dj a jazz music radio show in the 1950s, has a huge collection of jazz oldies, and can usually tell by listening who's playing what when.

Chad has been a trout fisherman since he was a boy. He spends a month in Colorado each summer fishing 18 hours a day and sleeping the other six. (Last year we got a Three Stooges postcard from him—they were out of Fur-Bearing Trout and Jackalopes cards—saying, "Your story is out in *Omni* at the newsstand in Lake City. I don't care.") He was president of the Texas Chapter of Trout Unlimited, where he fought various state river authorities who weren't releasing enough water during the summer to keep the trout alive. When Chad told them what was happening, the men at the hatcheries said, "Why don't we just shovel these fish into buckets of boiling water and save everybody trouble?"

We're in the middle of a Chad Oliver renaissance for the simple reason that good work wins out eventually. A couple of years ago *Mists of Dawn* came back into print, and recently both *Shores of Another Sea* and *Another Kind* have been reprinted. A German publisher is considering bringing out the entire Oliver *oeuvre* in a language Chad can't read. Better than that, "Ghost Town" was on the 1984 final Nebula ballot, for the simple reason that it was so good even the writers noticed.

Chad is fond of quoting a review he read about one of the old farts in the field years ago that went something like "...and this man is still writing stories even though he is fifty-five years old!"

As you read this Chad is turning sixty-one. He's been talking about himself posthumously for ten years. ("We didn't need phasers, we had ray-guns then!")

This bibliography is not so much a summation of forty years of creative work as it is a way-station. What is most wonderful about this is not where Chad Oliver has been, but where he's going.

("Colorado in July," he would say.)

Happy Bibliography-liay, Chad.

—Howard Waldrop

A CHAD OLIVER CHRONOLOGY

1928   Born on March 30th in Cincinnati, Ohio, son of Dr. Symmes F. Oliver and Winona Neuman.

1942   The first of many fan letters written by Oliver to the SF pulps appears in *Famous Fantastic Mysteries* (September).

1943   The Oliver family moves to Crystal City, Texas.

1946   Oliver graduates from Crystal City High School. Later this year, he begins attending the University of Texas, Austin.

1948   First fictional work, "The Imperfect Machine," published in *Texas Literary Quarterly*.

1950   First professional sale, "The Boy Next Door," is sold to *The Magazine of Fantasy and Science Fiction* (but is the third actually to appear in print). First professional fiction publication, "Land of Lost Content," appears in *Super Science Stories*.

1951   Receives a B.A. degree in the Plan II (Honors) Program, at the University of Texas, Austin; while working on his master's degree there, he serves as a freshman English teacher (through 1952).

1952   Awarded a Master's degree in English, with a minor in anthropology, at the University of Texas, Austin. His thesis, *They Builded a Tower*, is one of the earlier studies of science fiction at the master's level, and may have been the first to focus on magazine science fiction. Marries Betty Jane Jenkins on Nov. 1, 1952, at Los Angeles; the reception is held at the home of Forrest J Ackerman. Oliver's first novel, *The Mists of Dawn*, is published in cloth by John C. Winston Co. for its SF series for young adults.

1953   Works as a teaching assistant for the Department of Anthropology at the University of California, Los Angeles (through 1954), while working on his doctorate.

1954   The author's second novel, *Shadows in the Sun*, is published by Ballantine Books in cloth and paper editions.

1955   Oliver returns to the University of Texas at Austin, where he is employed as an Instructor for the Department of Anthropology, teaching Introductory Physical Anthropology, Introductory Cultural Anthropology, Peoples of the New World, and American Indians North of Mexico (through 1959). The author's first collection of short fiction, *Another Kind*, is published by Ballantine Books.

1956   First child, Kimberly Francis, born November 4th at Austin, Texas.

1957   *The Winds of Time*, Oliver's third SF novel, is published by Doubleday & Co.

1958   Works as a disk jockey for radio station KHFI in Austin, hosting the show, *American Jazz*, through 1959.

1959   Promoted to Assistant Professor of Anthropology at Austin (on leave, 1960-62, to conduct field work). Oliver's most anthologized short story, "Transfusion," is published in *Astounding* (June).

1960   Serves as visiting Assistant Professor of Anthropology at the University of California, Riverside, teaching Language and Culture, Introductory Cultural Anthropology, and The American Indian and Comparative Religion; also teaches at UCLA during the Summer session. A fourth science fiction novel, *Unearthly Neighbors*, is published in paperback by Ballantine Books.

1961   Oliver is awarded a Ph.D. degree in Anthropology from the University of California, Los Angeles, submitting a dissertation entitled *Ecology and Cultural Continuity As Factors in the Social Organization of the Plains Indians*. Later this same year, he works as a Research Anthropologist for the National Science Foundation in Kenya (through 1962), studying the culture and ecology of two Kamba tribal settlements, Ngelani, a farming community, and Kilungu, a herding community. Begins working on his novel, *The Wolf Is My Brother*, and notes that his Indians sound more like the Kambas than American aboriginals.

1963   Promoted to Associate Professor of Anthropology at Austin, and adds teaching responsibilities in African Cultures South of the Sahara, Social Organization, and Sociocultural Evolution.

1966   Oliver's fiftieth published short story, "Just Like a Man," published in *Fantastic* (July).

1967   Receives a Spur Award from the Western Writers of America for Best Novel of the Year, for *The Wolf Is My Brother*, published earlier in the year by New American Library. Oliver is appointed Chairman of the Department of Anthropology at Austin (through 1971), and adds teaching responsibilities for Man, Society, and Culture (Plan II), and Indians of the Plains.

1968   Son, Glen Chadwick, born February 3rd at Houston, Texas. Oliver is promoted to full Professor at Austin.

1971   The author's second collection of short fiction, *The Edge of Forever: Classic Anthropological Science Fiction Stories*, is published in cloth by Sherbourne Press of Los Angeles; and his fifth SF novel, *The Shores of Another Sea*, appears later the same year from New American Library.

1974   *Two Horizons of Man: Parallels and Interconnections Between Anthropology and Science Fiction*, is presented at the symposium Alternative Anthropological Futures, and then published by them as a short monograph.

1975   *The Winds of Time* is reprinted in Avon's SF Rediscovery Series.

1976   Oliver's sixth SF novel, *Giants in the Dust*, is published by Pyramid Books.

1980   Awarded the Harry Ransom Award for Teaching Excellence (Ransom was Oliver's committee chair for his master's degree, and later became the Chancellor of the University of Texas at Austin). Named Chairman of the Department of Anthropology for the second time (through 1985).

1981   Publishes a textbook of anthropology, *The Discovery of Humanity: An Introduction to Anthropology* (Harper & Row).

1982   Receives the University of Texas Presidential Award for Teaching Excellence, for outstanding contributions to the Plan II (i.e., Honors) Program at Austin.

1984   Two early novels, *Unearthly Neighbors* and *Shores of Another Sea*, are reprinted in the Classics of Modern Science Fiction Series from Crown Publishers.

1985   *Chad Oliver: A Preliminary Bibliography*, by Hal W. Hall, is published. A third novel, *Shadows in the Sun*, is reprinted in the Classics of Modern Science Fiction Series.

1986   Oliver's first western short story, "Take a Left at Bertram," in published in *The Best of the West* by Doubleday.

1988   *The Wolf Is My Brother*, Oliver's award-winning western novel, is reprinted in paperback by Bantam Books.

1989   Returns to full-time teaching; completes the manuscript for his second western novel, *Broken Eagle*, which is released by Bantam Books in August. *The Work of Chad Oliver: An Annotated Bibliography & Guide*, the first complete guide to the author's works, is published.

A.

BOOKS

A1. **Mists of Dawn.** Philadelphia: John C. Winston Co., 1952, 208
   p., cloth. $2.00. Jacket and end-papers by Alex Schomburg.
   [science fiction novel]

 b. as: *Mark's Reis in Het Verleden.* Hoorn, Netherlands: West
    Friesland, 1953, 188 p., cloth (?). Translated by Bauke An-
    dreisz. Not seen. [Dutch]
 c. London: Hutchinson, 1954, 240 p., cloth. Price: 7/6.
 d. as: *Chikyu no Yoake.* Tokyo: Sekisen-sha, 1956, 216 p., cloth
    (?). Translated by Asao Shima. Not seen. [Japanese]
 e. as: *Menschheitsdammerung.* Rastatt: Artur Moewig Verlag,
    1966,   p., paper. Terra #484. Not seen. [German]
 f. Boston: Gregg Press, May 1979, xv, 208 p., cloth. Introduc-
    tion by Oliver. Dust jacket by Michael Symes.
 g. as: *Menschheitsdammerung* (?). Germany: Artur Moewig,
    p., paper (?). Not seen. [German]

Mark Nye, in an accident involving a time machine, is precip-
itated into the past, and must survive in the time of Neanderthal and Cro-Magnon man until his time machine recharges
and a return home is possible. On a foraging expedition, he is
taken in by a Cro-Magnon group. He participates in mammoth
hunts, battles, and Cro-Magnon life in general before returning
to his own time.

The Winston science fiction series was packaged together
with uniform end sheets by well-known SF artist, Alex Schom-
burg, for the adolescent market, and achieved wide circulation
and acceptance. Oliver here demonstrates his knowledge of anthropology through a fictional setting, something which was to
become a hallmark of his later SF and western novels.

SECONDARY SOURCES & REVIEWS:

1. *Chicago Sunday Tribune* (November 16, 1952): 5.
2. Conklin, Groff. *Galaxy Science Fiction* 5 (March, 1953):
   111.

3. *Kirkus Reviews* 20 (September 1, 1952): 561.
4. *Library Journal* 77 (November 15, 1952): 2015.
5. *Magazine of Fantasy & Science Fiction* 4 (January, 1953): 89.
6. Miller, P. Schuyler. *Astounding Science Fiction* 53 (August, 1953): 145-146.
7. *New York Times Book Review* (November 16, 1952): 28.
8. *New York Tribune Herald Book Review* (October 26, 1952): 10.
9. *San Francisco Chronicle* (November 16, 1952): 12.
10. *Space Science Fiction* 2 (July, 1953): 92-93.
11. *Space Stories* 2 (April, 1953): 127-128.

A2. **Shadows in the Sun.** New York: Ballantine Books, December 1954, 152 p., cloth. $2.00. [science fiction novel]

ab. New York: Ballantine Books, December 1954, 152 p., paper. Published simultaneously. Stock #91, 35¢.

ac. New York: A Ballantine Books, January 1968, 152 p., paper. Stock #U2857, 50¢. Includes: "A Note to Teachers and Parents." A Ballantine Bal-Hi Book (for the school trade).

b. London: Max Reinhardt, 1955, 184 p., cloth. Jacket painting by E. B. Mudge-Marriott. Price: 9/6.

c. as: *Ombres sur le Soleil.* Paris: Denoël, 1956, 257 p., paper. Presence du Futur #12. Translated by Claude Elsen. [French]

d. [Garden City, NY: Science Fiction Book Club, 1957], 192 p., cloth. Title page reads: New York: Ballantine Books. Bound in burnt orange boards with black lettering.

e. as: *Das Licht aller Sonnen.* West Germany: _____, 1960, p., paper (?). Not seen. [German]

f. as: *Sombras en el Sol.* Buenos Aires: Fabril, 1964, p., paper. Fantasciencia #8. There may have been an earlier edition of this book published in 1957. Not seen. [Spanish]

g. London: A Four Square Book, 1965, 190 p., paper. Stock #1177, price 3/6.

h. as: *Taiyô no Kage.* Tokyo: Hayakawa Shobo, 1965, 177 p., paper. Translated by Obi Fusa. Not seen. [Japanese]

i. as: *Ombre nel Sole.* Italy: Ponzoni, 1966, p., paper. I Romanzi del Cosmo #193. Not seen. [Italian]

j. as: *Die vom Anderen Stern.* München: Wilhelm Heyne Verlag, 1967, 157 p., paper. TB Science Fiction #3090. Translated by Christiane Nogly. Not seen. [German]

k. as: *Vultos Sobre o Sol.* Rio de Janeiro: Expressão e Cultura, 1974, 175 p., paper. Not seen. [Portuguese]

1. New York: Crown Publishers, 1985, xvii, 207 p., cloth. Classics of Modern Science Fiction #9. Jacket painting by Michael Booth. Includes a new Foreword by Isaac Asimov, a new Introduction by George Zebrowski, and a new Afterword by Oliver himself.

Paul Ellery, on an anthopological research field trip to Jefferson Springs, Texas, begins to notice certain inconsistencies, culminating in the realization that no resident of this 137-year-old town has lived there more than 15 years. Further investigation reveals that the residents are alien colonists. Ellery confronts the leaders, and is invited to join the aliens, but chooses to remain a resident of Earth.

An earlier version of this novel was written as a novella, put aside, and finally published in 1976 as "Community Study."

SECONDARY SOURCES AND REVIEWS:

1. *Amazing Stories* 29 (May, 1955): 1114.
2. *American Anthropologist* 57 (October 1955): 1109-1110.
3. *Argentine Science Fiction Review* 1 (April, 1969): 12.
4. *Authentic Science Fiction* no. 54 (February, 1955): 127.
5. *Authentic Science Fiction* no. 66 (February, 1956): 152-153.
6. Boucher, Anthony. *The Magazine of Fantasy & Science Fiction* 8 (April, 1955): 81.
7. Boucher, Anthony. *The Magazine of Fantasy & Science Fiction* 15 (October, 1958): 52.
8. *Fantastic Universe* 2 (January, 1955): 126-127.
9. *Galaxy Science Fiction* 9 (February, 1955): 108.
10. Gerson, V. *New York Times Book Review* (December 5, 1944): 40.
11. *Inside* no. 7 (January, 1955): 27.
12. *Library Journal* 79 (October 1, 1954): 1818.
13. *Magazine of Fantasy & Science Fiction* 8 (March, 1955): 70-73.
14. Miller, P. Schuyler. *Astounding Science Fiction* 55 (May, 1955): 149.
15. *New Worlds Science Fiction* no. 43 (January, 1956): 126-127.
16. *Science Fiction Quarterly* 3 (May, 1955): .
17. Slater, Kenneth. *Nebula Science Fiction* no. 16 (March, 1956): 101-102.

A3.   **Another Kind: Science-Fiction Stories.** New York: Ballantine Books, 1955, 170 p., cloth. $2.00. Jacket painting by Richard Powers. [science fiction collection]

   ab. New York: Ballantine Books, 1955, 170 p., paper. Stock number #113, 35¢. Issued simultaneously with the cloth edition. Cover by Richard Powers.

   b.   as: *Menschen auf Fremden Sterner.* München: Artur Moewig Verlag, 1965, 98 p., paper. Terra SF #98. Not seen. [German]

The author's first collection of short stories, several of them previously published.

CONTENTS: "Mother of Necessity" (1955; see B31); "Rite of Passage" (1954; see B22); "Scientific Method" (1955; see B21); "Night" (1955; see B28); "Transformer" (1954; see B25); "Artifact" (1955; see B30); "A Star Above It" (1955; see B32).

Various binding states exist for the hardcover edition, including red cloth with black lettering, and ivory cloth with red lettering. Some hardcovers feature a dustwrapper by Richard Powers (the same painting which is used as the cover for the paperback edition).

SECONDARY SOURCES AND REVIEWS:

1.   *Amazing Stories* 30 (February, 1956): 118.
2.   Boucher, Anthony. *Magazine of Fantasy & Science Fiction* 10 (January, 1956): 96.
3.   Boucher, Anthony. *Magazine of Fantasy & Science Fiction* 10 (March, 1956): 121-122.
4.   Boucher, Anthony. *Magazine of Fantasy & Science Fiction* 15 (October, 1958): 52.
5.   *Galaxy Science Fiction* 11 (March, 1956): 97.
6.   *Inside and SF Advertiser* (November, 1955): 24.
7.   Knight, Damon. *Science Fiction Stories* 6 (March, 1956): 95, 116, 140.
8.   Miller, P. Schuyler. *Astounding Science Fiction* 57 (April, 1956): 148-149.
9.   *New York Times* (October 23, 1955): 30.
10. Santesson, Hans. *Fantastic Universe* 4 (January, 1956): 128.

A4.   **The Winds of Time.** Garden City, NY: Doubleday & Co., April 1957, 192 p., cloth. $3.95. Jacket design by Dick Shelton. [science fiction novel]

b. [Garden City, NY: Science Fiction Book Club, 1957], 192 p.,
    cloth. Jacket design by Dick Shelton. Title page reads: Gar-
    den City, NY: Doubleday & Co.
c. New York: Pocket Books, December 1958, 153 p., paper.
    Stock #1222, 35¢. Cover painting by Richard Powers.
d. as: *Le Spirali del Tempo.* Italy: Mondadori, 1958,   p., pa-
    per. Urania #179 and 488. Not seen. [Italian]
e. as: *Toki no Kaze.* Tokyo: Hayakawa Shobo, 1962, 201 p., pa-
    per. Translated by Taro Koizumi. There may have been an
    earlier edition of this book in 1960. Not seen. [Japanese]
f. as: *Veter Vremeni.* Moskva: Mir, 1965, 255 p., cloth (?).
    Translated by N. Rahmanova. Not seen. [Russian]
g. New York: Avon Equinox, 1975, 153 p., paper. SF Rediscov-
    ery Series #10. Stock #23887. Cover by Gray Morrow.
h. as: *Les Vents du Temps.* Paris: Opta, 1979,   p., cloth (?).
    Galaxie-bis #61. Not seen. [French]
hb. as: *Les Vents du Temps.* Paris: J'Ai Lu, 1980, 224 p., paper.
    Science Fiction Fantaisie #116. Not seen. [French]

Wes Chase is captured by a group of aliens, who have been in
suspended animation since being marooned on Earth some
10,000 years ago. The aliens need a technological base to re-
build their spacecraft, but Earth is not advanced enough to
provide that technology. Chase and the aliens work out a solu-
tion to their problem.

SECONDARY SOURCES AND REVIEWS:

1. Boucher, Anthony. *Magazine of Fantasy & Science Fiction*
    13 (July, 1957): 93.
2. Carter, Lin. *Inside Science Fiction* (October, 1957): 25.
3. *Delap's Fantasy and Science Fiction Review* (August, 1975):
    28-29.
4. *Galaxy Science Fiction* 14 (September, 1957): 105-106.
5. *Houston Chronicle* (April 7, 1957): 35.
6. *Infinity Science Fiction* 2 (October, 1957): 107-108.
7. *Locus* no. 175 (June 24, 1975): 4.
8. Miller, P. Schuyler. *Astounding Science Fiction* 60
    (October, 1957): 154.
9. Miller, P. Schuyler. *Astounding Science Fiction* 63 (April,
    1959): 150.
10. Santesson, Hans. *Fantastic Universe* 8 (August, 1957): 112.
11. *Science Fiction Review Monthly* no. 5 (July, 1975): [17]. ˙˙
12. *Venture Science Fiction* 1 (July, 1957): 79.

A5.   **Unearthly Neighbors.** New York: Ballantine Books, 1960, 144
       p., paper. Stock #365K, 35¢. [science fiction novel]

  b.   as: *Senhores do Sonho.* Rio de Janeiro: GRD, 1964, 150 p.,
       paper (?). Translated by Erasmo C. Giacometti. Not seen.
       [Portuguese]
  c.   as: *Bruder unter Fremder Sonne.* München: Wilhelm Heyne
       Verlag, 1964, 155 p., paper. Translated by Werner Kortwich.
       Reprinted in 1972 and 1977. Not seen. [German]
  d.   as: *Isei no Rinjin Tachi.* Tokyo: Hayakawa Shobo, 1967, 180
       p., paper. Translated by Adachi Kaede. Not seen. [Japa-
       nese]
  e.   as: *Das Grosse Warten.* München: Wilhelm Heyne Verlag,
       1963, 153 p., paper. Translated by Charlotte Winheller.
       Reprinted in 1970. Not seen. [German]
  f.   New York: Crown Publishers, 1984, xiv, 208 p., cloth. Clas-
       sics of Modern Science Fiction #8. Includes a new Intro-
       duction by George Zebrowski, a new Foreword by Isaac Asi-
       mov, and an Afterword by Chad Oliver.

Dr. Monte Stewart and a scientific crew are involved in a study
of an alien native culture, the Merdosi, on their native planet.
The study is progressing well, when the tribe suddenly and
inexplicably attacks and kills all but two of the team. Stewart,
with the help of one Merdosi, discovers the reason for the attack, prevents the possibility of reprisals, and allows contact
and the study to continue.

SECONDARY SOURCES AND REVIEWS:

  1.   *Amazing Science Fiction Stories* 34 (June, 1960): 134.
  2.   *Analog Science Fact & Fiction* 66 (October, 1960): 168-
       169.
  3.   Flood, Leslie. *New Worlds Science Fiction* no. 94 (May,
       1960): 126, 128.
  4.   *Kirkus Reviews* 52 (July 15, 1984): 661.
  5.   Pohl, Frederik. *Worlds of If* 10 (September, 1960): 90.

A6.   **Ecology and Cultural Continuity As Contributing Factors in
       the Social Organization of the Plains Indians,** by Symmes C.
       Oliver. Berkeley, CA: University of California Press, 1962,
       90 p., paper. University of California Publications in
       American Archaeology and Ethnology, v. 48, no. 1. [nonfic-
       tion]

b. in: *Man in Adaptation*, edited by Yehudi A. Cohen. Chicago: Aldine, 1968, cloth?, p. 243-262.

c. New York: Kraus Reprint Co., 1971, 90 p., cloth.

d. in: *Man in Adaptation, Second Edition* (?), edited by Yehudi A. Cohen. Chicago: Aldine, 1974, cloth?, p. 302-322.

SECONDARY SOURCES AND REVIEWS:

1. *Ethnohistory* 10 (Spring, 1963): 88-89. (J. Ewers)
2. Tomasson, R. *American Sociological Review* 29 (June, 1964): 475-476.

A7. **The Wolf is My Brother.** New York: A Signet Book, New American Library, January 1967, 144 p., paper. Stock #D3081, 50¢. [Western novel]

b. London: Herbert Jenkins, 1968, 190 p., cloth. Jacket painting by S. R. Boldero.

c. London: Mayflower, 1969, 156 p., paper.

d. as: *La Tribù Ribelle.* Milano: Casa Editrice Sonzogno, 1971, 187 p., paper (?). Not seen. [Italian]

e. as: *Der Wolf Mein Bruder.* München: Wilhelm Heyne Verlag, 1970, 144 p., paper. Not seen. [German]

f. as: *Vargen är Min Broder.* Stockholm: Wennerberg, 1972, 143 p., paper (?). Translated by Lennart Allen. Not seen. [Swedish]

f. Toronto, New York: Bantam Books, 1988, 170 p., paper. Cover by Frank McCarthy. Includes an excerpt at the end of the book from Oliver's (then) forthcoming novel, *Broken Eagle.*

Col. William Curtis and his 12th Cavalry face the challenge of keeping the High Plains of Texas safe from Indian attacks. Fox Claw, Comanche warrior and Chief, watches his people dying in both body and spirit, and tries to rally them for one last time. The collision course the two follow provide a poignant look at the point of view of both the Indians and the Army in the conflict over future control of the Texas Panhandle.

An Author's Note appears on p. 143-144 of the first edition. The Signet edition went through at least four printings.

A8. **The Shores of Another Sea.** New York: A Signet Book, New American Library, February 1971, 159 p., paper. Stock #T4526, 75¢. Cover art by Bob Pepper. [science fiction novel]

b. London: Victor Gollancz, 1971, 191 p., cloth.
c. as: *No Limiar de Novos Mundos.* Rio de Janeiro: Editura Expressão e Cultura, 1971, 164 p., paper (?). Translated by José Sanz. Not seen. [Portuguese]
d. as: *Le Rive di un Altro Mare.* Italy: Mondadori, 1972,   p., paper (?). Urania #599. Reprinted in 1982. Not seen. [Italian]
e. as: *Die Affenstation.* München: Wilhelm Heyne Verlag, 1973 128 p., paper. TB Science Fiction #3340. Not seen. [German]
f. New York: Crown Publishers, 1984, xii, 214 p., cloth. Classics of Modern Science Fiction #3. Jacket painting by Michael Booth. With a new introduction by George Zebrowski, and a Foreword by Isaac Asimov.
g. London: Robson, 1985, xii, 214 p., cloth.
h. Richmond, Victoria: Greenhouse Publications, 1985, xii, 214 p, cloth (?). Classics of Modern Science Fiction #3. Not seen.

Dr. Royce Crawford, resident anthropologist at a baboonery in East Africa, confronts an increasingly dangerous series of events, as first baboons, and then humans, are "possessed" by aliens from a mysterious fireball. After his daughter is captured by the aliens, Crawford captures four of the baboons/aliens, and arranges a barter of the captives for his daughter.

SECONDARY SOURCES AND REVIEWS:

1. *Analog Science Fiction/Science Fact* 104 (October, 1984): 150.
2. *Book Report* 3 (May, 1984): 37.
3. *Books & Bookmen* 17 (October, 1971): 50-51.
4. Budrys, Algis. *Magazine of Fantasy & Science Fiction* 67 (August, 1984): 36.
5. *Fantasy Review* 7 (August, 1984): 20.
6. *Kirkus Reviews* 51 (December 15, 1983): 1275.
7. *Locus* (June 25, 1971): 3.
8. *Los Angeles Times Book Review* (June 10, 1984): 4.
9. Marsh, B. *Ash-Wing* no. 9 (December, 1971): 29. A letter of comment from Hal Hall appeared in *Ash-Wing* no. 10 (June, 1972): 50-51.

10. *Milwaukee Journal* (March 4, 1984):   . Reprinted in: *NewsBank Review of the Arts & Literature* 10 (April, 1984): Card 71, p. F9.
11. *Observer* (November 21, 1971): 32.
12. Patten, Fred. *Son of the WSFA Journal* no. 49 (February 4, 1972): 3, 10.
13. Pauls, Ted. *Moebius Trip* no. 11 (December, 1971): 23.
14. *Publishers Weekly* 199 (January 4, 1971): 58.
15. Sakers, D. *Baltimore Sun* (March 11, 1984): 9.
16. *Science Fiction Review* 13 (May, 1984): 23.
17. *Science-Fiction Studies* 11 (July, 1984): 200-203.
18. *Washington Post Book World* (April 22, 1984): 11.

A9.   **The Edge of Forever: Classic Anthropological Science Fiction Stories**, by Chad Oliver, anonymously edited by William F. Nolan. Los Angeles: Sherbourne Press, August 1971, 305 p., cloth. [science fiction collection]

b.   as: *Fronteiras da Eternidade*. Rio de Janeiro: Expressão e Cultura, 1973, 279 p., paper (?). Not seen. [Portuguese]

c.   as: *Al Filo do lo Eterno*. Buenos Aires: Andromeda, 1976 (?), p., paper (?). Colección Ciencia-Ficción. Not seen. [Spanish]

This collection of six previously published stories by Oliver includes a biographical introduction by Nolan, commentary by the author, and a bibliography of Oliver's SF. See also Item A25 in *The Work of William F. Nolan: An Annotated Bibliography & Guide*, by Boden Clarke and James Hopkins (San Bernardino, CA: The Borgo Press, 1988, p. 32-33).

CONTENTS: "Transfusion" (1959; see B47); "A Friend to Man" (1951; see B4); "Field Expedient" (1955; see B27); "The Ant and the Eye" (1953; see B18); "First to the Stars" (1952; see B11); "Didn't He Ramble?" (1957; see B36); "Afterthoughts" (commentary by Oliver); "The Worlds of Chad Oliver: A Biographical Introduction," by William F. Nolan; "Chad Oliver's Collected Science Fiction: A Basic Checklist," by William F. Nolan.

SECONDARY SOURCES AND REVIEWS:

1. *Magazine of Fantasy & Science Fiction* 43 (November, 1972): 17.
2. Miller, P. Schuyler. *Analog Science Fiction/Science Fact* 90 (January, 1973): 163-164.

3. *Publishers Weekly* 200 (July 12, 1971): 68.

A10. **Two Horizons of Man: Parallels and Interconnections Between Anthropology and Science Fiction.** Austin, TX: The Author, 1974, 19 p., paper. [nonfiction]

"A paper to be presented November 21, 1974, at the Symposium entitled, 'Alternative Anthropological Futures: Anthropological Theory and Science Fiction,' at the 73rd meeting of the American Anthropological Association, Mexico City, November 19-24, 1974."

A11. **Giants in the Dust.** New York: Pyramid Books, March 1976, 142 p., paper. Stock #V3670, ISBN 0-515-03670-9, $1.25. [science fiction novel]

b. as: _____. Rastatt: Artur Moewig Verlag, 1984, p., cloth (?). Not seen. [German]

Varnum is chosen as the leader of a colonization effort designed to regain mankind's lost drives. To insure that the same old culture problems do not develop, all of the colonists have their memories of their previous lives erased. The settlers rapidly pass through various anthropological stages, reaching the stone age quickly, and inventing agriculture in less than a decade.

SECONDARY SOURCES AND REVIEWS:

1. *Publishers Weekly* 209 (February 12, 1976): 104.
2. Shiner, L. *Tales From Texas* 2 (July, 1976): [1].

A12. **The Discovery of Humanity: An Introduction to Anthropology.** New York, Hagerstown: Harper & Row, 1981, xxi, 407 p., cloth. [nonfiction]

An illustrated textbook of anthropology designed for college-level courses.
    CONTENTS: Preface: Who Needs a Textbook? 1. A Point of View; 2. How to Recognize an Anthropologist; 3. Cutting Up the Pie: The Subdivisions of Anthropology; 4. Primate, Meet Primate: Introducing the Chimpanzee; 5. The Other Side of the Mirror: Field Studies of Chimpanzees; 6. Communication

with Chimpanzees: A Dialogue Begins; 7. The Talking Animal: Language and Why It Matters; 8. Culture: What We Learn and Why; 9. How It Works: Some Characteristics of Cultural Systems; 10. Prehistory: The Roads Behind Us; 11. The Early Development of Anthropology; 12. The Later Development of Anthropology; 13. Living Together: Introducing Social Organization; 14. Who Goes Where: Principles of Marriage, Descent, and Residence; 15. Kin Groups: The Family, the Lineage, and the Clan; 16. A World of Relatives: The Difference Kinship Makes; 17. Hunting for the Food Collectors: Introducing Political Organization; 18. Let's Get Organized: Middle-Range Societies and States; 19. The Supernatural; 20. How to Do It: Supernatural Practitioners and Supernatural Concepts; 21. Cultural Change; Epilogue: Over the Hill or Over the Horizon?; Glossary; Name Index; Subject Index.

A13. **Broken Eagle.** New York, Toronto: Bantam Books, August 1989, 296 p., paper. ISBN 0-553-27997-1, $3.95. Cover art by Lou Glanzman. [western novel]

Oliver's second western is set in the northern American plains of 1876, where all trails lead to the Little Big Horn Valley. Crazy Horse, Sitting Bull, Broken Eagle, and the Sioux and Cheyenne Indians who follow them, have gathered at a common encampment there. General George A. Custer, Major Reno, Captain Singletary, and the rest of the Seventh Cavalry race across the plains to attack. The story unfolds through the eyes of Broken Eagle and Singletary, leading up to that fateful afternoon of June 25, 1876, when Custer finally meets his Waterloo.

The book includes an "Author's Note" identifying the historical personality upon which the character of John Singletary is based, and notes several sources which cover the action described in the novel.

B.

SHORT FICTION

B1. "The Imperfect Machine," in *Texas Literary Quarterly* 1 (Summer, 1948): 21-25.

B2. "Land of Lost Content," in *Super Science Stories* 7 (November, 1950): 74-85.

   b. *Super Science Stories* (U.K.) no. 3 (1950): 43-53.
   c. *An Argosy Special: Science Fiction,* edited by Lou Sahadi. New York: Popular Publications, 1977, paper, p. 10-14, 63-65.

B3. "Blood Star," by Chad Oliver and Garvin Berry, in *Super Science Stories* 7 (January, 1951): 48-61.

B4. "Let Me Live in a House," in *Universe Science Fiction* no. 4 (March, 1951): 27-51.

   b. *Authentic Science Fiction* no. 70 (June, 1956): 106-139.
   c. *Science Fiction Terror Tales,* edited by Groff Conklin. New York: Gnome Press, 1955, cloth, p. 233-262.
  cb. *Science Fiction Terror Tales,* edited by Groff Conklin. New York: Pocket Books, 1955, paper, p. 233-262.
  cc. *Science Fiction Terror Tales,* edited by Groff Conklin. New York: Pocket Books, 1969, paper, p. 233-262.
   d. as: "A Friend to Man," in *The Edge of Forever: Classic Anthropological Science Fiction Stories.* Los Angeles: Sherbourne Press, 1971, cloth, p. 87-121.

B5. "The Boy Next Door," in *Magazine of Fantasy & Science Fiction* 2 (June, 1951): 44-50.

   b. *Human??????,* edited by Judith Merril. New York: Lion Books, 1954, paper, p. 17-25.
   c. *The Eureka Years: Boucher and McComas's Magazine of Fantasy & Science Fiction, 1949-1954,* edited by Annette Pelz McComas. Toronto, New York: Bantam Books, 1982, paper,

p. 128-138. Includes a letter from Oliver to Editor Anthony Boucher.

B6.   "Reporter," in *Fantastic Story Magazine* 3 (Fall, 1951): 107-112, 116.

B7.   "The Edge of Forever," in *Astounding Science Fiction* 48 (December, 1951): 61-81.

  b.   as: "Soglia dell'Eternita," in *Scienza Fantastica* 7 (1953): . Not seen. [Italian]

B8.   "Subversives," in *Startling Stories* 25 (February, 1952): 74-84.

  b.   as: "Win the World," in *Looking Forward: An Anthology of Science Fiction*, edited by Milton Lesser. New York: Beechhurst Press, 1953, cloth, p. 56-66.

B9.   "Lady Killer," in *Startling Stories* 25 (March, 1952): 91-97.

B10.   "Blood's a Rover," in *Astounding Science Fiction* 49 (May, 1952): 9-48.

  b.   *Astounding Science Fiction* (U.K.)   (October, 1952): 133- .
  c.   *Operation Future*, edited by Groff Conklin. New York: Permabooks, 1955, paper, p. 177-229.
  d.   *Deep Space: Eight Stories of Science Fiction*, edited by Robert Silverberg. Nashville, TN: Thomas Nelson, 1973, cloth, p. 1-53
  db. *Deep Space: Eight Stories of Science Fiction*, edited by Robert Silverberg. [Garden City, NY: Science Fiction Book Club, 1973 (?)], cloth, p. 1-52. Title page reads: Nashville: Thomas Nelson.
  dc. *Deep Space: Eight Stories of Science Fiction*, edited by Robert Silverberg. New York: A Dell Book, 1974, paper, p. 9-69.

B11.   "Stardust," in *Astounding Science Fiction* 49 (July, 1952): 123-155.

  b.   *Astounding Science Fiction* (U.K.)   (December, 1952): 135- .
  c.   *Adventures in the Far Future*, edited by Donald A. Wollheim. New York: Ace Books, 1954, paper, p. 51-86.
  d.   as: "First to the Stars," in *The Edge of Forever: Classic Anthropological Science Fiction Stories*. Los Angeles: Sherbourne Press, 1971, cloth, p. 229-276.

e. as: "Sternenstaub," in *Piloten Durch Zeit und Raum*, edited by Ronald Hahn. Enigen: Ensslin & Labin Verlag, 1983, cloth (?), p. 139-171. Not seen. [German]

B12. **"Fires of Forever,"** in *Science Fiction Adventures* 1 (November, 1952): 5- 43.

b. *American Science Fiction* Series (Australia) (April 1953): 1-28.

B13. **"Final Exam,"** in *Fantastic* 1 (November-December, 1952): 56-66.

b. *Amazing Stories* 40 (December, 1965): 53-63.
c. *An ABC of Science Fiction*, edited by Tom Boardman, Jr. London: A Four Square Book, 1966, paper, p. 105-116.
cb. *An ABC of Science Fiction*, edited by Tom Boardman, Jr. New York: Avon, 1968, paper, p. 117-127.
d. *The Best from Fantastic*, edited by Ted White. New York: Manor Books, 1973, paper, p. 125-137.
db. *The Best from Fantastic*, edited by Ted White. London: Robert Hale, 1976, cloth, p. 125-137.

B14. **"Technical Advisor,"** in *The Magazine of Fantasy & Science Fiction* 4 (February, 1953): 30-40.

b. *Crossroads in Time*, edited by Groff Conklin. Garden City, NY: Permabooks, 1953, paper, p. 199-210.
c. *The Hollywood Nightmare: Tales of Fantasy and Horror from the Film World*, edited by Peter Haining. London: Macdonald & Co., 1970, cloth, p. 227-239.
cb. *The Hollywood Nightmare: Tales of Fantasy and Horror from the Film World*, edited by Peter Haining. New York: Taplinger Publishing Co., 1971, cloth, p. 227-239.
d. as: "Le Conseiller Technique," in *Fiction* no. 15 (Février, 1955): . Not seen. [French]

B15. **"Judgment Day,"** in *Science Fiction Adventures* 1 (March, 1953): 71-89.

B16. **"Shore of Tomorrow,"** in *Startling Stories* 29 (March, 1953): 90-112.

b. *Popular Science Fiction* (Australia) 1 (November, 1953): .
c. *Tomorrow's Universe*, edited by H. J. Campbell. London: Hamilton & Co., 1953, cloth, p. 140-184. Published simultaneously in trade paperback under the Panther imprint.

B17.   "**Anachronism,**" in *The Magazine of Fantasy & Science Fiction* 4 (April, 1953): 52-56.

B18.   "**The Ant and the Eye,**" in *Astounding Science Fiction* 51 (April, 1953): 104-136.

   b.   *Stories for Tomorrow: An Anthology of Modern Science Fiction*, edited by William Sloane. New York: Funk and Wagnalls, 1954, cloth, p. 353-388.
  bb.   *Stories for Tomorrow: An Anthology of Modern Science Fiction*, edited by William Sloane. London: Eyre & Spottiswood, 1955, cloth, p. 263-298.
   c.   *The Edge of Forever: Classic Anthropological Science Fiction Stories.* Los Angeles: Sherbourne Press, 1971, cloth, p. 177-228.

B19.   "**Hardly Worth Mentioning,**" in *Fantastic* 2 (May-June, 1953): 96-140.

   b.   *Fantastic Stories* 15 (March, 1966): 22-55, 150-160.

B20.   "**Life Game,**" in *Thrilling Wonder Stories* 42 (June, 1953): 108-122.

   b.   *The Pseudo-People: Androids in Science Fiction*, edited by William F. Nolan. Los Angeles: Sherbourne Press, 1965, cloth, p. 56-75.
  bb.   *Almost Human: Androids in Science Fiction*, edited by William F. Nolan. London: Souvenir Press, 1966, cloth, p. 56-78.
  bc.   *The Pseudo-People: Androids in Science Fiction*, edited by William F. Nolan. New York: A Berkley Medallion Book, 1967, paper, p. 71-93.
  bd.   *Almost Human: Androids in Science Fiction*, edited by William F. Nolan. London: Mayflower-Dell, 1967, paper, p. 67-87.
  be.   as: "Gioco Delloa Vita," in *Quasi Umani: Gli Androidi e i Robot nella Fantascienza*, edited by William F. Nolan. Milano: Sugar Editore, 1967, paper, p. 94-120. Pocket di F.S. #490. [Italian]
  bf.   as: "   ," in *Die Anderen Unter Uns*, edited by William F. Nolan. Offenburg: Joseph Melzer, 1967, cloth, p. 109-148. [German]
  bg.   as: "   ," in *Die Anderen Unter Uns*, edited by William F. Nolan. München: Wilhelm Heyne Verlag, 1968, paper, p.   . Not seen. [German]

bh. as: "Gioco Delloa Vita," in *Quasi Umani*, edited by William F. Nolan. Milano: Longanesi, 1975, paper, p. 86-112. [Italian]

B21. **"Hands Across Space,"** in *Science Fiction Plus* 1 (August, 1953): 36-41.

b. as: "Scientific Method," in *Another Kind*. New York: Ballantine Books, 1955, cloth, p. 60-74. Published simultaneously in mass market paperback.

c. *Science Fiction Monthly* (Australia) no. 7 (March 1956): . Not seen.

d. *The Human Zero and Other Science Fiction Masterpieces*, edited by Sam Moskowitz and Roger Elwood. New York: Tower Books, 1967, paper, p. 106-124.

e. as: "Primo Contatto," in _____. Italy: La Tribuna, 1974, paper (?), p. . Galassia #196. Not seen. [Italian]

B22. **"Rite of Passage,"** in *Astounding Science Fiction* 53 (April, 1954): 49-86.

b. *Another Kind*. New York: Ballantine Books, 1955, cloth, p. 15-60. Published simultaneously in mass market paper.

c. *Seven Come Infinity*, edited by Groff Conklin. Greenwich, CT: Fawcett Gold Medal, 1966, paper, p. 239-288.

B23. **"Of Course,"** in *Astounding Science Fiction* 53 (May, 1954): 52-63.

b. *The Best Science-Fiction Stories and Novels 1955*, edited by T. E. Dikty. New York: Frederick Fell, 1955, cloth, p. 57-72.

c. *Apeman Spaceman: Anthropological Science Fiction*, edited by Harry Harrison and Leon E. Stover. Garden City, NY: Doubleday & Co., 1968, cloth, p. 298-310.

cb. *Apeman Spaceman: Anthropological Science Fiction*, edited by Harry Harrison and Leon E. Stover. London: Rapp & Whiting, 1968, cloth, p. 298-310.

cc. *Apeman Spaceman: Anthropological Science Fiction*, edited by Harry Harrison and Leon E. Stover. New York: A Berkley Medallion Book, 1970, paper, p. 316-329.

cd. *Apeman Spaceman: Anthropological Science Fiction*, edited by Harry Harrison and Leon E. Stover. Harmondsworth, Middlesex: Penguin Books, 1969?, paper, p. . Not seen.

d. *Sociology Through Science Fiction*, edited by John W. Milstead, Martin Harry Greenberg, Patricia S. Warrick, and Joseph D. Olander. New York: St. Martin's Press, 1974, cloth, p. 105-118. Published simultaneously in trade paperback.

e. *Science Fiction and Fantasy: 26 Classic and Contemporary Stories*, edited by Fred Obrecht. Woodbury, NY: Barron's Educational Series, 1977, cloth, p. 139-153.

B24. **"Any More at Home Like You,"** in *Star Science Fiction Stories #3*, edited by Frederik Pohl. New York: Ballantine Books, 1954, cloth, p. 130-144. Issued simultaneously in mass market paperback.

b. *New Worlds Science Fiction* no. 39 (September, 1955): 77-89.
c. *Science Digest* 92 (September, 1984): 66-70.

B25. **"Transformer,"** in *The Magazine of Fantasy & Science Fiction* 7 (November, 1954): 70-81.

b. *Another Kind.* New York: Ballantine Books, 1955, cloth, p. 92-106. Published simultaneously in mass market paperback.
c. as: "Les Habitants de la Ville-Jouet," in *Fiction* no. 23 (Octobre, 1955): 95-107. [French]
d. *Man Against Tomorrow*, edited by William F. Nolan. New York: Avon, 1965, paper, p. 135-148.
e. *Isaac Asimov Presents The Great SF Stories: 16 (1954)*, edited by Isaac Asimov and Martin H. Greenberg. New York: DAW Books, 1987, paper, p. 211-226.

B26. **"Controlled Experiment,"** in *Orbit Science Fiction* 1 (November/December, 1954): 58-70.

b. *Space Station 42 and Other Stories* [an anonymously edited anthology]. London, New York: Satellite Books, March 1958, paper, p. 16-29. Satellite Series #212.

B27. **"Field Expedient,"** in *Astounding Science Fiction* 54 (January, 1955): 59-114.

b. *The Hidden Planet: Science-Fiction Adventures on Venus*, edited by Donald A. Wollheim. New York: Ace Books, 1959, paper, p. 7-56.
c. *The Edge of Forever: Classic Anthropological Science Fiction Stories.* Los Angeles: Sherbourne Press, 1971, cloth, p. 122-176.

B28. **"Night,"** in *Worlds of If* 5 (March, 1955): 40-53.

b. *Another Kind.* New York: Ballantine Books, 1955, cloth, p. 74-96. Published simultaneously in mass market paperback.

B29. **"Last Word,"** by Chad Oliver and Charles Beaumont, in *The Magazine of Fantasy & Science Fiction* 8 (April, 1955): 120-127. Claude Adams Series #1.

   b. *The Best From Fantasy and Science Fiction, Fifth Series*, edited by Anthony Boucher. Garden City, NY: Doubleday & Co., 1956, cloth, p. 245-256.
  bb. *The Best From Fantasy and Science Fiction, Fifth Series*, edited by Anthony Boucher. New York: Ace Books, 1961, paper, p. 242-253.
   c. as: "Claude à Travers le Temps," in *Fiction* no. 33 (Août, 1956): 73-82. Translated by Bruno Martin. [French]
   d. *Evil Earths: An Anthology of Way-Back-When Futures*, edited by Brian W. Aldiss. London: Weidenfeld & Nicolson, 1976, cloth, p. 5-15.
  db. *Evil Earths: An Anthology of Way-Back-When Futures*, edited by Brian W. Aldiss. London: Futura Publications, An Orbit Book, 1976, paper, p. 5-15.
  dc. *Evil Earths: An Anthology of Way-Back-When Futures*, edited by Brian W. Aldiss. New York: Avon, 1979, paper, p. 5-15.
  dd. as: "   ," in *Terre Pericolose*, edited by Brian W. Aldiss. Milano: Fanucci, 1979, cloth, p.   . Not seen. [Italian]
  de. as: "   ," in *Wrede Werelden*, edited by Brian W. Aldiss. Amsterdam: Centripress, 1980, paper, p.   . Not seen. [Dutch]
  df. as: "   ," in *Titan-22*, edited by Brian W. Aldiss. München: Wilhelm Heyne Verlag, 1984, paper, p.   . Not seen. [German]

B30. **"Artifact,"** in *The Magazine of Fantasy & Science Fiction* 8 (June, 1955): 108-126.

   b. *Another Kind*. New York: Ballantine Books, 1955, cloth, p. 107-130. Published simultaneously in mass market paperback.
   c. *New Worlds Science Fiction* no. 46 (April, 1956): 105-125.
   d. as: "L'Objet," in *Fiction* no. 29 (Avril, 1956): 3-23. [French]

B31. **"Mother of Necessity,"** in *Another Kind*, by Chad Oliver. New York: Ballantine Books, 1955, cloth, p. 1-14. Published simultaneously in mass market paperback.

   b. *Great Science Fiction by Scientists*, edited by Groff Conklin. New York: Collier, 1962, paper, p. 241-256.

bb. as: "Madre della Necessità," in *Raconti di Fantascienza Scritta dagli Scineziati*, edited by Groff Conklin. Milano: Rizzoli, 1965, paper (?), p. . Not seen. [Italian]

c. *Above the Human Landscape: A Social Science Fiction Anthology*, edited by Willis E. McNelly and Leon E. Stover. Pacific Palisades, CA: Goodyear Publishing Co., 1972, cloth, p. 27-38. Published simultaneously in trade paperback.

d. *Science Fiction A to Z: A Dictionary of the Great S.F. Themes*, edited by Isaac Asimov, Martin H. Greenberg, and Charles G. Waugh. Boston: Houghton Mifflin Co., 1982, cloth, p. 557-570.

B32. "A Star Above It," in *Another Kind*, by Chad Oliver. New York: Ballantine Books, 1955, cloth, p. 130-170. Published simultaneously in mass market paperback.

b. as: "Fugo nel Tempo," in _____. Italy: Vallecchi, 1961, paper (?), p. . I Gabbiani #1. Not seen. [Italian]

B33. "I, Claude," by Chad Oliver and Charles Beaumont, in *The Magazine of Fantasy & Science Fiction* 10 (February, 1956): 99-112. Claude Adams Series #2.

b. as: "Claude l'Invincible," in *Fiction* no. 34 (Septembre, 1956): 29-44. Translated by Richard Chamet. [French]

c. *Laughing Space: Funny Science Fiction*, edited by Isaac Asimov and J. O. Jeppson. Boston: Houghton Mifflin Co., 1982, cloth, p. 361-373.

B34. "North Wind," in *The Magazine of Fantasy & Science Fiction* 10 (March, 1956): 53-70.

b. as: "Le Vent du Nord," in *Fiction* no. 36 (Novembre, 1956): 62-83. Translated by Regine Vivier. [French]

c. *A Wilderness of Stars: Stories of Man in Conflict with Space*, edited by William F. Nolan. Los Angeles: Sherbourne Press, 1969, cloth, p. 224-253.

cb. *A Wilderness of Stars: Stories of Man in Conflict with Space*, edited by William F. Nolan. London: Victor Gollancz, 1970, cloth, p. 224-253.

cc. *A Wilderness of Stars: Stories of Man in Conflict with Space*, edited by William F. Nolan. Newton Abbot, Devon: Science Fiction Book Club, 1971, cloth, p. 224-253.

cd. *A Wilderness of Stars: Stories of Man in Conflict with Space*, edited by William F. Nolan. New York: A Dell Book, 1971, paper, p. 196-221.

ce. *A Wilderness of Stars: Stories of Man in Conflict with Space*, edited by William F. Nolan. London: Corgi Books, 1972, paper, p. 182-204. Reprinted in 1980.

d. *The Far-Out People: A Science Fiction Anthology*, edited by Robert Hoskins. New York: A Signet Book, New American Library, 1971, paper, p. 14-35.

e. as: "Vento del Nord," in *Robot* 6 (Settembre, 1976): 124-143. [Italian]

B35. **"Guests of Chance,"** by Chad Oliver and Charles Beaumont, in *Infinity Science Fiction* 1 (June, 1956): 4-22.

b. *Night Ride and Other Journeys*, by Charles Beaumont. New York: Bantam Books, 1960, paper, p. 111-126.

B36. **"Didn't He Ramble?"** in *The Magazine of Fantasy & Science Fiction* 12 (April, 1957): 118-127.

b. *The Magazine of Fantasy & Science Fiction* (Australia) no. 14 (August, 1958): . Not seen.

c. as: "Départ en Beauté," in *Fiction* no. 56 (Juillet, 1958): 27-37. Translated by Bruno Martin. [French]

d. *The Best Science-Fiction Stories and Novels, Ninth Series*, edited by T. E. Dikty. Chicago: Advent:Publishers, 1958, cloth, p. 85-96.

e. *The Edge of Forever: Classic Anthropological Science Fiction Stories*. Los Angeles: Sherbourne Press, 1971, cloth, p. 277-293.

B37. **"Between the Thunder and the Sun,"** in *The Magazine of Fantasy & Science Fiction* 12 (May, 1957): 3-45.

b. *The Best from Fantasy and Science Fiction, Seventh Series*, edited by Anthony Boucher. Garden City, NY: Doubleday & Co., 1958, cloth, p. 120-181.

bb. *The Best from Fantasy and Science Fiction, Seventh Series*, edited by Anthony Boucher. New York: Ace Books, 1962, paper, p. 115-172.

c. as: "Entre le Tonnerre et le Soleil," in *Fiction* no. 94 (Septembre, 1961): 3-47. Translated by Arlette Rosenblum. [French]

B38. **"The Wind Blows Free,"** in *The Magazine of Fantasy & Science Fiction* 13 (July, 1957): 3-25.

b.   as: "Le Vent Souffle où il Veut," in *Fiction* no. 68 (Juillet, 1959): 96-119. Translated by Arlette Rosenblum. [French]

c.   *A Sea of Space*, edited by William F. Nolan. New York: Bantam Books, 1970, paper, p. 13-39.

cb. *A Sea of Space*, edited by William F. Nolan. London: Corgi Books, 1980, paper, p. 13-39.

B39. **"Rewrite Man,"** in *The Magazine of Fantasy & Science Fiction* 13 (September, 1957): 60-77.

b.   as: "Paternité," in *Fiction* no. 61 (Décembre, 1958): 105-124. Translated by Roger Durand. [French]

B40. **"Pilgrimage,"** in *The Magazine of Fantasy & Science Fiction* 14 (February, 1958): 5-18.

b.   as: "Culbute dans le Temps," in *Fiction* no. 65 (Avril, 1959): 73-88. Translated by Roger Durand. [French]

c.   *Special Wonder: The Anthony Boucher Memorial Volume of Fantasy and Science Fiction*, edited by J. Francis McComas. New York: Random House, 1970, cloth, p. 326-341.

cb. *Special Wonder, Volume 2: The Anthony Boucher Memorial Volume of Fantasy and Science Fiction*, edited by J. Francis McComas. New York: Beagle Books, 1970, paper, p. 153-172.

B41. **"Space Horde,"** in *Amazing* 32 (February, 1958): 88-104.

b.   *The Most Thrilling Science Fiction Ever Told* no. 4 (1966): 4-20.

c.   as: "Chi ci Salvera?" in _____. Milano: Mondadori, 1973, paper, p. . Il Passo dell'Ignoto. Not seen. [Italian]

B42. **"Cowardice of Tom Royce,"** in *Saturday Evening Post* 230 (April 5, 1958): 31, 75, 77, 80. [Western]

b.   as: "Man Alone," in *John Bull* (U.K.) 104 (1958): 16-19.

B43. **"Guardian Spirit,"** in *The Magazine of Fantasy & Science Fiction* 14 (April, 1958): 5-39.

b.   *Venture Science Fiction* (U.K.) no. 24 (August, 1965): . Not seen.

c.   as: "L'Esprit Gardien," in *Fiction* no. 143 (Octobre, 1965): 9-50. Translated by Pierre Billon. [French]

d.   as: "The Marginal Man," in *3 to the Highest Power*, edited by William F. Nolan. New York: Avon, 1968, paper, p. 113-158.

db.   as: "The Marginal Man," in *3 to the Highest Power*, edited by William F. Nolan. London: Corgi Books, 1971, paper, p. 97-139. Reprinted in 1980.

B44.   **"Last of the Wild Ones,"** in *Argosy Magazine* 347 (August, 1958): 25-27, 82-85. [Western]

B45.   **"From Little Acorns,"** in *Satellite Science Fiction* 3 (February, 1959): 48-52, 64.

B46.   **"One That Got Away,"** in *The Magazine of Fantasy & Science Fiction* 16 (May, 1959): 41-50.

b.   *Venture Science Fiction* (U.K.) no. 13 (September, 1964): . Not seen.

B47.   **"Transfusion,"** in *Astounding Science Fiction* 63 (June, 1959): 44-77.

b.   *Worlds of When: Five Short Novels*, edited by Groff Conklin. New York: Pyramid Books, 1962, paper, p. 9-46.

c.   as: "Tempo dell'Nomo," in _____. Milano: Mondadori, 1963, paper, p. . Urania #324. Not seen. [Italian]

d.   *The Edge of Forever: Classic Anthropological Science Fiction Stories*. Los Angeles: Sherbourne Press, 1971, cloth, p. 33-86.

e.   *Anthropology Through Literature: Cross Cultural Perspectives*, edited by James P. Spradley and George McDonough. Boston: Little, Brown & Co., 1973, paper (?), p. 5-36.

f.   *Analog's Golden Anniversary Anthology*, edited by Stanley Schmidt. New York: Longmeadow Press, Davis Publications, 1981, cloth, p. 229-260.

g.   *Creations: The Quest for Origins in Story and Science*, edited by Isaac Asimov, George Zebrowski, and Martin Greenberg. New York: Crown Publishers, 1983, cloth, p. 249-285.

gb.   *Creations: The Quest for Origins in Story and Science*, edited by Isaac Asimov, George Zebrowski, and Martin Greenberg. London: Harrup, 1984, cloth, p. . Not seen.

h.   *Great Science Fiction: Stories by the World's Great Scientists*, edited by Isaac Asimov, Martin H. Greenberg, and Charles G. Waugh. New York: Donald I. Fine, 1985, cloth, p. 285-328.

B48. "The End of the Line," in *The Magazine of Fantasy & Science Fiction* 28 (January, 1965): 5-31.

b. as: "La Fin du Voyage," in *Fiction* no. 140 (Juillet, 1965): 10-45. Translated by Pierre Billon. [French]

c. *Once and Future Tales from The Magazine of Fantasy and Science Fiction*, edited by Edward L. Ferman. [Jacksonville, IL.]: Delphi Press, 1968, cloth, p. 75-112.

B49. "A Stick for Harry Eddington," in *The Magazine of Fantasy & Science Fiction* 29 (August, 1965): 81-95.

b. as: "Corps de Rechange," in *Fiction* no. 15 (Mai, 1966): 9-26. Translated by Yves Hersant. [French]

c. as: "Transferimento di Personalità," in _____. Milano: Mondadori, 1968, paper, p. . Urania #500. Not seen. [Italian]

d. *SF: Author's Choice 2*, edited by Harry Harrison. New York: A Berkley Medallion Book, 1970, paper, p. 155-158. Includes a lengthy new introduction by Oliver.

B50. "Just Like a Man," in *Fantastic Stories* 15 (July, 1966): 6-65.

B51. "Far From This Earth," in *The Year 2000: An Anthology*, edited by Harry Harrison. Garden City, NY: Doubleday & Co., 1970, cloth, p. 57-74.

ab. *The Year 2000: An Anthology*, edited by Harry Harrison. London: Faber & Faber, 1971, cloth, p. 57-74.

ac. *The Year 2000: An Anthology*, edited by Harry Harrison. New York: A Berkley Medallion Book, 1972, paper, p. 53-68.

b. *Themes in Science Fiction: A Journey into Wonder*, edited by Leo P. Kelley. New York: McGraw-Hill Book Co., 1972, paper, p. 47-59.

c. *Anthropology Through Science Fiction*, edited by Carol Mason, Martin Harry Greenberg, and Patricia S. Warrick. New York: St. Martin's Press, 1974, cloth, p. 201-215. Published simultaneously in trade paperback.

d. *American English Today: The Tools of English*, edited by Hans P. Guth and Edgar H. Schuster. New York: McGraw-Hill Book Co., 1975, paper (?), p. 251-252. Extract only.

B52. "King of the Hill," in *Again, Dangerous Visions: 46 Original Stories*, edited by Harlan Ellison. Garden City, NY: Doubleday & Co., 1972, cloth, p. 170-186 ab. *Again, Dangerous Visions: 46 Original Stories*, edited by Harlan Ellison. [Garden City, NY: Science Fiction Book Club, 1973 (?)], cloth, p. . Title page reads: Garden City, NY: Doubleday & Co. Not seen.

ac. *Again, Dangerous Visions: 46 Original Stories, Volume 1*, edited by Harlan Ellison. New York: A Signet Book, New American Library, 1973, paper, p. 197-216.

ad. *Again, Dangerous Visions: 46 Original Stories*, edited by Harlan Ellison. London & Sydney: Pan Books, 1973, paper, p. . Not seen.

b. *Catastrophes!*, edited by Isaac Asimov, Martin H. Greenberg, and Charles G. Waugh. New York: Fawcett Crest, 1981, paper, p. 176-192.

B53. "Second Nature," in *Future Quest*, edited by Roger Elwood. New York: Avon, 1973, paper, p. 35-70.

b. *The Gifts of Asti, and Other Stories of Science Fiction*, edited by Roger Elwood. Chicago: Follett Publishing Co., 1975, cloth, p. 106-135.

B54. "Shaka," in *Continuum 1*, edited by Roger Elwood. New York: G. P. Putnam's Sons, 1974, cloth, p. 76-103. Caravans #1.

ab. *Continuum 1*, edited by Roger Elwood. New York: A Berkley Medallion Book, 1975, paper, p. 62-84.

See also the comics adaptation (E1).

B55. "The Gift," in *Future Kin: Eight Science Fiction Stories*, edited by Roger Elwood. Garden City, NY: Doubleday & Co., 1974, cloth, p. 33-60.

b. as: "Dono," in _____. Milano: Mondadori, 1975, paper, p. . Urania #670. Not seen. [Italian]

B56. "Caravans Unlimited—Stability," in *Continuum 2*, edited by Roger Elwood. New York: G. P. Putnam's Sons, 1974, cloth, p. 82-113. Caravans #2.

ab. *Continuum 2*, edited by Roger Elwood. New York: A Berkley Medallion Book, 1975, paper, p. 60-83.

B57. "The Middle Man," in *Continuum 3*, edited by Roger Elwood. New York: Berkley Publishing Corp., 1974, cloth, p. 55-84. Caravans #3.

ab. *Continuum 3*, edited by Roger Elwood. New York: A Berkley Medallion Book, 1975, paper, p. 46-71.

B58. "Caravans Unlimited—Monitor," in *Continuum 4*, edited by Roger Elwood. New York: Berkley Publishing Corp., 1975, cloth, p. 62-88. Caravans #4.

ab. *Continuum 4*, edited by Roger Elwood. New York: A Berkley Medallion Book, 1976, paper, p. 57-80.

B59. "Community Study," in *Lone Star Universe: The First Anthology of Texas Science Fiction Authors*, edited by Geo. W. Proctor and Steven Utley. Austin, TX: Heidelberg Publishers, 1976, cloth, p. 51-79.

Originally written in the early 1950s, this story was put aside after being expanded into and published as the novel, *Shadows in the Sun.*

B60. "Meanwhile, Back on the Reservation," in *Analog Science Fiction/Science Fact* 101 (April 27, 1981): 86-101.

B61. "To Whom It May Concern," in *A Spadeful of Spacetime*, edited by Fred Saberhagen. New York: Ace Books, 1981, paper, p. 12-31.

B62. "Ghost Town," in *Analog Science Fiction/Science Fact* 103 (Mid-September, 1983): 10-27.

B63. "Take a Left at Bertram," in *The Best of the West*, edited by Joe R. Lansdale. Garden City, NY: Doubleday & Co., 1986, cloth, p. 14-22.

B64. "On Night at Medicine Tail," in *Westeryear*, edited by Edward Gorman. New York: M. Evans & Co., 1988, cloth, p. 172-185.

B65. "To Hell with Claude," by Charles Beaumont and Chad Oliver, in *Charles Beaumont: Selected Stories*, by Charles Beaumont. Arlington Heights, IL: Dark Harvest, 1988, cloth, p. 347-359.

An original story written by Oliver from notes made by Oliver and Beaumont before the latter's death (in 1967). Includes a new introduction by Oliver explaining how the story came to be written.

B66. "Old Four-Eyes," in *Synergy 4*, edited by George Zebrowski. San Diego: A Harvest/HBJ Original, Harcourt Brace Jovanovich, 1989, paper, p. 126-160.

Includes an introduction by the editor.

C.
NONFICTION

NOTE: Science fiction book reviews also appeared in the *Daily Texan* (University of Texas, Austin) and the *Austin American-Statesman* newspaper during the period 1955-1960. Oliver has no record of these publications.

C1. **"Ray Bradbury: The Martian Chronicler,"** in *Ray Bradbury Review*, edited by William F. Nolan. San Diego: William F. Nolan, January 1952, paper, p. 40-41. [criticism]

b. Los Angeles: Graham Press, 1988, cloth, p. 40-41.

C2. **"Science Fiction—What It Is and What It Isn't,"** in *Texas Ranger* 65 (October, 1952): 14-15. [criticism]

C3. **"What is Science Fiction?"** in *Inside/SF Advertiser* 6 (November, 1954): 22-24. [criticism]

C4. **"When Fiction Turns to Fact: We Live Together, or Die,"** in *Austin American* (October 25, 1957): 4. [current affairs]

An appraisal of the Sputnik flight then recently launched by the Russians. According to Bill Warren (*Austin Statesman*, Nov. 11, 1957), this column was "widely reprinted" in various Texas newspapers.

C5. **"The World of Man, by J. J. Honigmann,"** in *American Anthropologist 62 (August, 1960): 700-701. [review]*

C6. **"Readings in Anthropology, edited by M. J. Fried,"** in *American Anthropologist* 62 (August, 1960): 700-701. [review]

C7. **"Individuality, Freedom of Choice, and Cultural Flexibility of the Kamba,"** in *American Anthropologist* 67 (April, 1965): 421-428. [anthropology]

b. *The Individual and Culture*, edited by Mary Ellen Goodman. Homewood, IL: Dorsey Press, 1967, cloth (?), p. 172-173, 183-185.

c. *Variation and Adaptability of Culture: A Symposium on Some Results of the Culture and Ecology Project in East Africa*, presented at the 63rd annual meeting of the American Anthropological Association, Detroit, Mich., Nov. 20, 1964. No place: American Anthropological Association, [1964], paper (?), p. 33-34.

C8. **"Ecological Variation and Lineage Structure,"** in *Texas Journal of Science* 18 (May 20, 1966): 126-127. [anthropology]

C9. **"Afterthoughts,"** in *The Edge of Forever: Classic Anthropological Science Fiction Stories*, by Chad Oliver. Los Angeles: Sherbourne Press, 1971, cloth, p. 294-300. [autobiography]

C10. **"The Plains Indians as Herders,"** *Paths to the Symbolic Self: Essays in Honor of Walter Goldschmidt*, edited by James P. Loucky and Jeffery R. Jones. Los Angeles: Department of Anthropology, University of California, Los Angeles, 1976, paper, p. 35-43. [anthropology]

b. *Anthropology USA* 8 (1976): 35-43. Published simultaneously.

C11. **"Edmond Hamilton,"** in *Twentieth-Century Science-Fiction Writers*, edited by Curtis C. Smith. New York: St. Martin's Press, 1981, cloth, p. 243-244. [criticism]

b. *Twentieth-Century Science-Fiction Writers, Second Edition*, edited by Curtis C. Smith. Chicago & London: St. James Press, 1986, cloth, p. 315-317. Unchanged except for a couple of additions to Hamilton's bibliography.

C12. **"Ross Rocklynne,"** in *Twentieth-Century Science-Fiction Writers*, edited by Curtis C. Smith. New York: St. Martin's Press, 1981, cloth, p. 454. [criticism]

b. *Twentieth-Century Science-Fiction Writers, Second Edition*, edited by Curtis C. Smith. Chicago & London: St. James Press, 1986, cloth, p. 611. Unchanged.

C13. **"The Hills and the Plains: A Comparison of Two Kamba Communities,"** in *Culture and Ecology: Eclectic Perspectives*, edited by John G. Kennedy and Robert B. Edgerton. Washington, D.C.: American Anthropological Association, 1982, paper, p. 142-157. Special Publication, No. 15. [anthropology]

C14. "Afterword," in *Unearthly Neighbors*, by Chad Oliver. New York: Crown Publishers, 1984, cloth, p. 204-208. [autobiography]

C15. "Some Blues for a Trio," in *Texas, Our Texas*, edited by Brian A. Garner. Austin, TX: Eakin Press, 1984, cloth, p. 96-106. [autobiography]

C16. "Afterword," in *Shadows in the Sun*, by Chad Oliver. New York: Crown Publishers, 1985, cloth, p. 202-207. [autobiography]

C17. "Second Thoughts," in *Chad Oliver: A Preliminary Bibliography*, by Hal W. Hall. Bryan, TX: Dellwood Press, 1985, paper, p. 82-86. [autobiography]

b. *The Work of Chad Oliver: An Annotated Bibliography & Guide*, by Hal W. Hall. San Bernardino, CA: The Borgo Press, October 1989, cloth, p. 78-80. Published simultaneously in trade paperback. Slightly edited for this version.

C18. "Afterword," in *Trail of the Spanish Bit*, by Don Coldsmith. Toronto, New York: Bantam Books, 1987, paper, p. 210-214. Spanish Bit Saga #1. [afterword]

C19. "On Heinlein's Death," in *SFWA Bulletin* 22 (Summer, 1988): 14. [memorial]

C20. "Cavalier in Buckskin, by Robert Utley," in *Heritage* (1989): . [review]

D.

LETTERS

NOTE: Oliver penned a series of fan letters to the pulp SF magazines beginning at the age of fourteen, and continuing until he began publishing his own fiction in these publications.

D1. *Famous Fantastic Mysteries* 4 (September, 1942): 138.

D2. *Famous Fantastic Mysteries* 5 (December, 1942): 139.

D3. *Planet Stories* 2 (Winter, 1942): 128.

D4. *Super Science Stories* 4 (November, 1942): 47-48.

D5. *Fantastic Adventures* 4 (December, 1942): 236.

D6. *Super Science Stories* 4 (February, 1943): 6, 8.

D7. *Thrilling Wonder Stories* 24 (February, 1943): 118.

D8. *Fantastic Adventures* 5 (March, 1943): 229.

D9. *Planet Stories* 2 (March, 1943): 126.

D10. *Fantastic Adventures* 5 (April, 1943): 236-237.

D11. *Fantastic Adventures* 5 (May, 1943): 237-238.

D12. *Planet Stories* 2 (May, 1943): 121.

D13. *Thrilling Wonder Stories* 24 (June, 1943): 122-124.

D14. *Startling Stories* 4 (June, 1943): 122-123.

D15. *Captain Future* 5 (Summer, 1943): 125-126.

D16. *Planet Stories* 2 (Fall, 1943): 122-123.

D17. *Thrilling Wonder Stories* 25 (Fall, 1943): 123-124.

D18. *Captain Future* 6 (Winter, 1943): 120.

D19. *Planet Stories* 2 (Winter, 1943): 117-118.

D20. *Astounding Science Fiction* 31 (August, 1943): 156-158.

D21. *Fantastic Adventure* 5 (August, 1943): 206-207.

D22. *Astounding Science Fiction* 31 (November, 1943): 178.

D23. *Startling Stories* 10 (Winter, 1944): 115-116.

D24. *Fantastic Adventures* 6 (April, 1944): 205.

D25. *Captain Future* 6 (Spring, 1944): 123.

D26. *Startling Stories* 11 (Summer, 1944): 106.

D27. *Planet Stories* 2 (Spring, 1944): 119.

D28. *Thrilling Wonder Stories* 25 (Winter, 1944): 11, 114.

D29. *Startling Stories* 11 (Winter, 1945): 108-109.

D30. *Startling Stories* 12 (Spring, 1945): 104.

D31. *Thrilling Wonder Stories* 27 (Summer, 1945): 88-89.

D32. *Startling Stories* 12 (Fall, 1945): 120.

D33. *Planet Stories* 3 (Winter, 1945): 120.

D34. *Planet Stories* 3 (Summer, 1946): 123-124.

D35. *Thrilling Wonder Stories* 28 (Summer, 1946): 100-101.

D36. *Planet Stories* 3 (Fall, 1946): 121-122.

D37. *Planet Stories* 3 (Winter, 1946): 123-124.

D38. *Thrilling Wonder Stories* 28 (Winter, 1946): 8, 10.

D39. *Planet Stories* 3 (Spring, 1946): 120-121.

D40. *Startling Stories* 14 (Fall, 1946): 8, 10, 98.

D41. *Startling Stories* 14 (January, 1947): 10, 98.

D42. *Thrilling Wonder Stories* 29 (February, 1947): 96.

D43. *Startling Stories* 15 (March, 1947): 94.

D44. *Thrilling Wonder Stories* 30 (April, 1947): 98.

D45. *Startling Stories* 15 (May, 1947): 8.

D46. *Planet Stories* 3 (Winter, 1947): 120-121.

D47. *Startling Stories* 16 (November, 1947): 94.

D48. *Astounding Science Fiction* 40 (December, 1947): 156-157.

D49. *Planet Stories* 3 (Spring, 1947): 128.

D50. *Thrilling Wonder Stories* 30 (August, 1947): 100-101.

D51. *Thrilling Wonder Stories* 31 (December, 1947): 99-100.

D52. *Fantasy Book* no. 3 (1948): 62.

D53. *Planet Stories* 3 (Fall, 1948): 2, 120.

D54. *Startling Stories* 18 (September, 1948): 122.

D55. *Thrilling Wonder Stories* 31 (February, 1948): 94-95.

D56. *Thrilling Wonder Stories* 32 (August, 1948): 126-127.

D57. *Thrilling Wonder Stories* 33 (October, 1948): 155.

D58. *Startling Stories* 18 (January, 1949): 152.

D59. *Super Science Stories* 5 (April, 1949): 106.

D60. *Planet Stories* 4 (Spring, 1949): 125.

D61. *Super Science Stories* 5 (September, 1949): 122-123.

D62. *Thrilling Wonder Stories* 34 (June, 1949): 142-143.

D63. *Super Science Stories* 6 (May, 1950): 6, 8.

D64. *Astounding Science Fiction* 45 (June, 1950): 150-151.

D65. *Super Science Stories* 8 (April, 1951): 99-101.

D66. *Startling Stories* 23 (May, 1951): 152.

D67. *Planet Stories* 5 (January, 1952): 104.

E.

OTHER MEDIA

E1.   "Shaka" in *Starstream* no. 1 (1976): 56-65. Adaptation by Ed Summer, art by Adolfo Buylla. [Comic strip]

A comic strip adapted from Oliver's short story of the same name (see B54).

E2.   **Barrett, Neal, Jr., Aggiecon Roast.**   College Station, TX: Texas A&M University Library, n.d., audio cassette. Features Chad Oliver as a panelist.

F.
UNPUBLISHED WORKS

F1. **They Builded a Tower: The Story of Science Fiction.** Austin, TX: The University of Texas, Austin, 1952, 137 typed manuscript pages. Oliver's unpublished Master's Thesis.

G.
ABOUT THE AUTHOR
Monographs, Profiles, Critiques

NOTE: The *Daily Texan*, mentioned as the source publication of some of the profiles listed below, is the student-edited newspaper of the University of Texas, Austin. Many of the citations listed are taken from tear-sheets whose page numbers cannot be specified further.

G1. "PS's Feature Flash," by Chad Oliver, in *Planet Stories* 2 (Spring, 1944): 113. [autobiographical letter]

G2. "Chad's Friend Speaks," by Garvin Berry, in *Thrilling Wonder Stories* 29 (December, 1946): 102-103. [biographical letter]

G3. "It Was Champagne for Chad Oliver on 1 Nov 52...; Oliver Guest Speaker at World's First Class in SF Authorship...," by Forrest J Ackerman, in *Fantasy Times* 7 (November, 1952): 6. [news item]

G4. "Chad Oliver's Astounding Story 'The Edge of Forever' Has Been Sold to Television. Another Ackerman Deal," in *Fantasy Times* 8 (August, 1953): 4. [news item]

G5. "Faculty Gains Noted Writer," in *Daily Texan* (October 5, 1955): . Oliver returns to the University of Texas as an anthropology teacher. [news item]

G6. "Anthropology and Science Fiction Combine to Keep U. T. Prof Busy," by Lorraine Barnes, in *Austin Statesman* (October 16, 1955): . Includes photograph and caption. [profile]

G7. "Chad Oliver Has Had a Daughter, Kimberley...," by Forrest J Ackerman, in *National Fantasy Fan* 15 (February, 1956): unnumbered page. [news item]

G8.   "Troubled World's Answer Lies in Book Open to All," by Bill Warren, in *Austin Statesman* (November 11, 1957):   . [profile]

G9.   "Science Fiction Guides Oliver into Anthropology," by Pat Terry, in *Daily Texan* (November 22, 1957): 2. Illustrated with a caricature drawing of Oliver. [profile]

G10.   "Texas Prof: Science Fiction," in *Dallas News* (March 31, 1957): . [profile]

G11.   "Bits About Books," by Bill Warren, in *Austin Statesman* (June 23, 1957): . [interview]

G12.   "Children To Hear UT Prof," in *Austin Statesman* (November 2, 1958): . [news item]

G13.   "Author Speaker for Book Week," in *Austin American* (November 2, 1958): . [news item]

G14.   "Science Fiction Defended in Talk by Chad Oliver," in *Daily Texan* (September 15, 1959): . [news item]

G15.   "In Oliver Case 'Scholar, Writer' Vie," by Anita Brewer, in *Austin American-Statesman* (October 4, 1962): . Includes photograph of Oliver. [profile/interview]

G16.   "Dr. Chadwick Oliver...Will Speak...on His Observations in Kenya...," in *Daily Texan* (October 7, 1962): . [news item]

G17.   "Oliver Predicts Independence For Kenya in Next Two Years," in *Daily Texan* (October 10, 1962): . [news item]

G18.   "A Chad Oliver Science Fiction and Fantasy Index," by William F. Nolan, in *3 to the Highest Power*, edited by William F. Nolan. New York: Avon, 1968, paper, p. 159-160. [bibliography]

G19.   "Editor's Preface: Chad Oliver," by William F. Nolan, in *3 to the Highest Power*, edited by William F. Nolan. New York: Avon, 1968, paper, p. 109-112. [profile]

G20.   "Author Scientist Creates Fiction from Cultures," in *Daily Texan* (February 9, 1969): . [profile]

G21. "The Electric Bibliograph, II: Chad Oliver," by Mark Owings, in *WSFA Journal* no. 67 (June/July, 1969): 21-23. [bibliography]

G22. "Books Column," by Bill Warren, in *Austin American-Statesman* (September 21, 1969): Show World Section, T27. Includes photo of Oliver. [profile/interview]

G23. "The Worlds of Chad Oliver: A Biographical Introduction," by William F. Nolan, in *The Edge of Forever: Classic Anthropological Science Fiction Stories*, by Chad Oliver. Los Angeles: Sherbourne Press, 1971, cloth, p. 11-32.

G24. "Chad Oliver's Collected Science Fiction: A Basic Checklist," by William F. Nolan, in *The Edge of Forever: Classic Anthropological Science Fiction Stories*, by Chad Oliver. Los Angeles: Sherbourne Press, 1971, cloth, p. 301-305. [bibliography]

G25. [Introduction to] "King of the Hill," by Harlan Ellison, in *Again, Dangerous Visions*, edited by Harlan Ellison. Garden City, NY: Doubleday & Co., 1972, cloth, p. 170-171. [profile]

G26. "Chad Oliver: 'I've Been Interested in Science Fiction Since I Was 14,'" by Candy O'Keefe, in *Daily Texan* (November 2, 1972): . [profile]

G27. "OLIVER, (Chad)," in *Encyclopédie de l'Utopie des Voyages Extraordinaires de la Science Fiction*, by Pierre Versins. Lausanne: L'Age d'Homme, 1972, cloth, p. 641-642. [criticism]

G28. "Science Fiction Convention Underway," by Steve Goble, in *The Eagle* (Bryan-College Station, TX) (March 4, 1973): 2A. A brief mention accompanied by a two-column photo of Oliver. [news item]

G29. "Outdoors: Maybe Brown Trout Instead," by Russell Tinsley, in *Austin American-Statesman* (December 4, 1973): 28. Oliver on brown trout fishing. [interview]

G30. "Introduction: 'Far From this Earth'," in *Anthropology Through Science Fiction*, edited by Carol Mason, Martin H. Greenberg, and Patricia Warrick. New York: St. Martin's Press, 1974, paper, p. 201-202. [profile]

G31. "The Union Column," in *Daily Texan* (September 27, 1974): .
A calendar entry about a science fiction symposium, Oliver's
sandwich seminar on "At the Edge of Forever." [news item]

G32. "Chad Oliver: Professor and Dreamer," by Howard Waldrop, in
Austin Sun 1 (November 7-13, 1974): 8-10. [profile]

G33. "Plan II: Program Offers 'Alternate Route' to BA Degree," by
Mark Manroe, in *Daily Texan* (August 8, 1975): . Oliver's
Social Science 301 is a required course for Plan II majors.
[news item]

G34. "Chad Oliver," in *Who's Who in Science Fiction*, by Brian Ash.
London: Elm Tree Books, 1976, cloth, p. 159. Also: New
York: Taplinger Publishing Co., 1976, cloth, p. 159. [biography]

G35. "Introduction to 'Community Study'," by Chad Oliver, in *Lone
Star Universe*, edited by George W. Proctor and Steve Utley.
Austin, TX: Heidelberg, 1976, cloth, p. 52-53. Details the
writing of Oliver's story, "Community Study," and the reason
it was ultimately expanded into the novel, *Shadows in the
Sun*. [autobiography]

G36. "A Notable Problem: Here's $10, Give Me the Lecture Notes
for the Last 10 Classes," by Lee Kelly, in *Austin American-
Statesman* (February 27, 1978): Bl, B3. A one-sentence reference
to Oliver's course in anthropology. [news item]

G37. "Dr. Chad Oliver: Author, Anthropologist, Professor, Fisherman...,"
by Becky Slaughter, in *Daily Texan* (April 19, 1978):
16. A long interview/article, with photo of Oliver.
[profile/interview]

G38. "For Dean's position King, Oliver, Ross Vying," by Carl
Hoover, in *Daily Texan* (July 27, 1978). The nominees and
the selection process for a newly-vacated dean's position.
[news item]

G39. "UT Names Dr. Robert King First Dean of Liberal Arts," in
Houston Chronicle (August 14, 1978). Oliver was one of three
nominees for the dean position. [news item]

G40. "King Named Dean of New UT college," in *Austin American-
Statesman* (August 15, 1978): . Oliver was nominated for
the position. [news item]

G41. **"Chad Oliver,"** in *Science Fiction and Fantasy Literature, 1700-1974, with Contemporary Science Fiction Authors II*, by R. Reginald. Detroit: Gale Research Co., 1979, cloth, Vol. I, p. 395; Vol. II, p. 1023. [bio-bibliography]

G42. **"Chad Oliver,"** in *A Reader's Guide to Science Fiction*, by Baird Searles, Beth Meacham, and Michael Franklin. New York: Avon, 1979, paper, p. 136-137. [criticism]

G43. **"Oliver, Chad,"** by John Clute, in *The Science Fiction Encyclopedia*, edited by Peter Nicholls. Garden City, NY: Doubleday & Co., 1979, cloth, p. 435-436. [criticism]

G44. **"Interview,"** in *SumerMorn* no. 3 (Fall, 1979): 21-25. [interview]

G45. **"Oliver, (Symmes) Chad(wick),"** in *Lexikon der Science Fiction Literatur*, edited by Hans Joachim Alper. München: Wilhelm Heyne Verlag, 1979, paper, Vol. 1, p. 496-497. [bio-bibliography]

G46. **"Oliver, Chad,"** in *Who Goes There?*, by James A. Rock. Bloomington, IN: James A. Rock, 1979, paper, p. 109. [bibliography]

G47. **"Students Discuss Textbooks,"** in *Daily Texan* (October 1, 1979):   . Oliver to speak on "What Johnny Has to Read: The Autobiography of a Textbook." [news item]

G48. **"Chad Oliver,"** by Howard Waldrop, in *ArmadilloCon I Program Book*. Austin, TX: The Convention, [1979?], p. 13-14. [profile]

G49. **"Dr. Chad Oliver,"** by Steve Utley, in *ArmadilloCon I Program Book*. Austin, TX: The Convention, [1979?], paper, p. [15-16]. [profile]

G50. **"Shadows in the Sun,"** by Gary K. Wolfe, in *Survey of Science Fiction Literature*, edited by Frank N. Magill. Englewood Cliffs, NJ: Salem Press, 1979, cloth, Vol. 4, p.1898-1901. [criticism]

G51. **"Oliver Wins Teaching Prize,"** by Pete Szigaly, in *Austin American-Statesman* (May 19, 1980): B2. Oliver receives the

Ransom Award—Harry Ransom was Oliver's first English
teacher. [interview]

G52. **"Oliver Receives Ransom Award,"** by Martha Chamberlain, in
On Campus 7 (June, 1980): 12. [profile]

G53. **"Professor Receives Award,"** in *Daily Texan* (June 2, 1980):   .
Oliver receives the Harry Ransom Teaching Excellence
Award. [news item]

G54. **"Chad Oliver,"** by Michael Adams, in *Twentieth-Century American Science-Fiction Writers*, edited by David Cowart and
Thomas L. Wymer. Detroit: Gale Research Co., 1981, cloth,
Vol. 2, p. 60-65. The Dictionary of Literary Biography, Vol.
8. [criticism]

G55. **"Hub?"** by Harry Hurt III, in *Texas Monthly* 9 (February,
1981): 110-111. Includes photos of Chad Oliver. [profile]

G56. **"In support of King"** (Firing Line column), in *Daily Texan*
(April 27, 1981):   . A letter to the Editor, supporting the
Dean of Liberal Arts, signed by Oliver and fifteen others.
[letter]

G57. **"Convention to Honor Professor/Sci-Fi Writer,"** by Douglas
McLeod, in *Daily Texan* (October 2, 1981):   . An ArmadilloCon announcement and interview. [interview]

G58. **"Science Fiction Convention to Feature Renowned Authors,
'Real Bad' Cinema,"** by Douglas McLeod, in *Daily Texan*
(October 1, 1981):   . An ArmadilloCon III announcement,
with one paragraph about Oliver as its guest of honor. [news
item]

G59. **"Flawn Blames Red Tape for Restricting Freedom,"** by W.
Gardner Selby and Jodi Hooker, in *Daily Texan* (October 2,
1981):   . Includes one paragraph about a teaching excellence
award in the amount of $5,000. given to eight faculty mem-
bers, including Oliver. [news item]

G60. **"ArmadilloCon Brings Science Fiction to Austin,"** by Gary L.
Warren, in *Daily Texan* (October 5, 1981):   . Oliver was
Guest of Honor at ArmadilloCon III; includes photo. [profile]

G61. **"UT Writers Mix Work with Science Fiction,"** by Steven T.
Levine, in *Daily Texan* (November 11, 1981):   . About

Oliver and Ed Nather (of the UTA Astrophysics Department). [profile]

G62.   **The Chad Oliver Roast: Aggiecon XIII.** College Station, TX: Aggiecon XIII, 1982, audio cassette. [interview]

G63.   **"UT-ex Bruce Sterling: a Writer Driven by Sci-Fi,"** by Robert Wexler, in *Daily Texan* (June 28, 1982):   . Includes a one-line mention of Oliver as a "great eminence" or "padrone" of Austin SF writers, in an interview with Sterling. [interview]

G64.   **"Austin Writers Invade Universe of Science Fiction,"** by Kerry Gunnels, in *Austin American-Statesman* (May 24, 1983): Onward Section, 6-7. Includes photo of Oliver. [profile]

G65.   **"In Search of: Symmes Chadwick Oliver,"** by Bill Page, in *Gavelkind* 6 (August, 1983): 4-5. [humorous profile]

G66.   **"Biolog: Chad Oliver,"** by Jay Kay Klein, in *Analog Science Fiction/Science Fact* 102 (Mid-September, 1983): 28. [profile]

G67.   **"Interview,"** by John Peterson, in *Austin Chronicle* 4 (December 21, 1984): 16-17. [interview]

G68.   **"Our Past, Chad Oliver's Future: Teacher, Innovator, Inspiration,"** by Steve Utley, in *Austin Chronicle* 4 (December 21, 1984): 16-17. [profile]

G69.   **"Introduction,"** by George Zebrowski, in *Unearthly Neighbors*, by Chad Oliver. New York: Crown Publishers, 1984, cloth, p. xi-xiv. [criticism]

G70.   **"Introduction,"** by George Zebrowski, in *The Shores of Another Sea*, by Chad Oliver. New York: Crown Publishers, 1984, cloth, p. viii-xii. [criticism]

G71.   **Chad Oliver: A Preliminary Bibliography,** by Hal W. Hall. Bryan, TX: Dellwood Press, 1985, (vi), 86 p., paper. [bibliography]

G72.   **"Introduction,"** by Howard Waldrop, in *Chad Oliver: A Preliminary Bibliography*, by Hal W. Hall. Bryan, TX: Dellwood Press, 1985, paper, p. 1-4. [profile]

b. *The Work of Chad Oliver: An Annotated Bibliography & Guide*, by Hal W. Hall. San Bernardino, CA: The Borgo Press, October 1989, cloth, p. 5-7. Published simultaneously in trade paperback.

G73. **"Interview,"** by Hal W. Hall and Richard D. Boldt, in *Chad Oliver: A Preliminary Bibliography*, by Hal W. Hall. Bryan, TX: Dellwood Press, 1985, paper, p. 50-81. [interview]

b. as: "An Interview with Chad Oliver," in *The Work of Chad Oliver: An Annotated Bibliography & Guide*, by Hal W. Hall. San Bernardino, CA: The Borgo Press, October 1989, cloth, p. 60-80. Published simultaneously in trade paperback. Edited for this version.

G74. **"Introduction,"** by George Zebrowski, in *Shadows in the Sun*, by Chad Oliver. New York: Crown Publishers, 1985, cloth, p. vii-xvii. [criticism]

G75. **"Chad Oliver,"** by Hal W. Hall, in *The New Encyclopedia of Science Fiction*, edited by James Gunn. New York: Harper & Row, 1988, cloth, p. 339. [criticism]

G76. **"University of Texas Plots to Be Great—Not Just Good,"** by Linda Austin. An uncited article, possibly from the *Dallas Times Herald*; one paragraph quotes Oliver regarding hindrances to UT advancement. [news item]

G77. **"UT Prof Gets Space Offer,"** by Betty MacNabb (On Research Column), in *Austin American-Statesman* (no date): . Margaret Mead sends Oliver a letter requesting possible projects on the cultures of space explorer units; some biographical details. [news item]

G78. **The Work of Chad Oliver: An Annotated Bibliography & Guide,** by Hal W. Hall. Bibliographies of Modern Authors, No. 12. San Bernardino, CA: The Borgo Press, October 1989, 88 p., cloth. Published simultaneously in trade paperback. [bibliography]

H.
ABOUT THE AUTHOR
News Releases

NOTE: uncited items are from the the University of Texas News and Information Service, Austin, Texas; copies are located in the Barker Collection, the University of Texas, Austin, Library.

H1. 3/28/57. On the release of *The Winds of Time.*

H2. 6/23/60. Oliver to spend 1960/61 academic year in California learning language of Ugandan natives in preparation for research expedition.

H3. 4/5/63. Oliver collection of East African artifacts on exhibit at Texas Memorial Museum.

H4. 2/19/65. Member of Texas Institute of Letters.

H5. 9/20/68. Oliver promoted to Professor.

H6. 12/4/72. Chairs session on science fiction at meeting of American Studies Association of Texas.

H7. 1/16/75. Speaks on "Two Horizons for Man: Some Parallels and Inter-Connections Between Anthropology and Science Fiction."

H8. 9/2/75. Runner-up for Jean Holloway Award for Teaching Excellence.

H9. 4/5/79. Lectures at program on art of the American West at Laguna Gloria Art Museum.

H10. 9/25/79. Gives talk on "What Johnny Has to Read."

H11. 5/1/80. Oliver as Ransom award winner.

H12. 10/1/81. Receives teaching excellence award for outstanding contributions to Plan II program.

H13. 4/2/81. Receives 1980 Ransom award.

H14. 3/7/83. Death of Dr. Ellen Brennan of the Anthropology Department, with Oliver's comments.

I.

HONORS AND AWARDS

I1. Spur Award, Best Western Novel of the Year, Western Writers of America, 1967, for *The Wolf Is My Brother*.

I2. Harry Ransom Award for Teaching Excellence, University of Texas at Austin, 1980.

I3. Presidential Award, University of Texas at Austin, 1982, for outstanding contributions to the Plan II (i.e., Honors) Program.

J.

MISCELLANEA

J1.   FANZINES. *The Moon Puddle*, Vol. I, No. 1, June 1948. Chad Oliver and Garvin Berry, Publishers. CONTENTS: "A Home for Luminescent Goldfish," by David H. Keller (p. 3-4); "Simians, Swords, and Supermen," by L. Sprague de Willy (p. 5-8); "The Last of the Lensmen," by E. E. Jones, Ph.D. (p. 22-23); "The Amoral Affectations of Henry Kuttner" (p. 31-37. Departments include: Puddle Poets; Ghosties, Ghouls, and Garvin (autobiographical); The Library of Ghu (reviews); Rusty Nails (letters); Creep, Chaddo (autobiographical).

    Oliver's first and only fanzine issue, *Moon* was published in an edition of fifty copies, all of them mailed to potentially interested fans and pros.

J2.   EDUCATION. Oliver received his bachelor's degree in 1951 from the University of Texas, Austin; his master's degree (in English) in 1952, from the same institution; and his Ph.D. (in Anthropology) in 1961, from the University of California at Los Angeles, with a dissertation entitled *Ecology and Cultural Continuity As Factors in the Social Organization of the Plains Indians.*

J3.   CAREER. Beginning in 1951, Austin has worked almost continually as a college teacher in anthropology at the University of Texas, Austin, successively as Instructor (1951-52, 1955-59), Assistant Professor (1959-62), Associate Professor (1963-68), and Professor (1968-DATE); he served two stints as Chairman of the Department of Anthropology there, from 1967-71 and 1980-85. In addition, he served as a teaching assistant (1953-54) and Visiting Assistant Professor (1960) for the Anthropology Department of UCLA, and an Assistant Professor of Anthropology at the University of California, Riverside (1960). He has also worked as a disk jockey for radio station KHFI in Austin, hosting a program on American jazz (1958-59), and as a Research Anthropologist for the National Science Foundation in Kenya (1961-62).

J4.   **CATALOGING DATA.** In the Library of Congress classification scheme, Oliver's main entry is "Oliver, Chad, 1928- "; his author number is PS3565.L458, and his bibliography number is Z8642.76.

AN INTERVIEW WITH CHAD OLIVER

Conducted by Hal W. Hall and Richard D. Boldt

BOLDT: As a fan, you wrote many letters to the magazines—which you might rather forget.

OLIVER: First of all, maybe I'd better say this—that I don't really want to forget those letters. They're kind of embarrassing to go back and read now—but, after all, you can't be held responsible for everything you said when you were fourteen-years-old. They meant a great deal to me at one period of my life, because when I was a kid I was nuts about sports and things of that kind. I was very active up until I got rheumatic fever when I was a child. I was very sick for a long time. All I had were books to read. I used to lie up in my bed in a two-storey house, and look out the window and see all these kids going down to play ball, and I couldn't go with them. All I had were the magazines and the letters I wrote. I can remember the desperate anxiety, waiting for the magazine to come out to see if my letter had appeared in print; if it had, it just made my day. I really think it would be ungrateful to go back now and say, it was just a mistake of my youth, because silly as they were, they were important to me then. But this doesn't really answer your question.

I was born in Cincinnati on March 30, 1928. My father was a doctor—a surgeon. My mother had been a nurse. She met my father when she was working professionally. In the full process of time, I appeared. I was still living in Cincinnati at the time I first discovered SF—actually I had read it long before I knew what it was. I began reading Jules Verne along about the fourth grade—and thought he was great. Then I hit H. G. Wells. I was also a Burroughs nut. I read everything Edgar Rice Burroughs ever wrote. I was particularly knocked out by the Martian series—I guess most kids were—I read *A Princess of Mars*, in which the hero gets to Mars by just going out and looking yearningly up at the Red Planet! I'm sure every kid who ever read Burroughs tried that. I've often thought what an utter disaster it would have been if it had worked—you'd suddenly wake up, a weak,

pimply thirteen-year-old boy standing there on Mars, sur-
rounded by all these fantastic things, including women who
lay eggs.

So I read Burroughs, and even got a letter from him
once, when he was kind enough to respond to a letter I wrote.
But let me back up a bit—I was an omnivorous reader, of
every book I could get my hands on, as well as the pulp
magazines. I read them all—well, almost all. I subscribed to
G8 And His Battle Aces and *Daredevil Aces* and *The Spider*
and *The Shadow* and *Doc Savage*, and all those things. My
pet was G8—looking back now I can see why—because Robert
J. Hogan's stories were terrific, filled with a wild, almost
"baroque" imagination. They're real science fiction, but were
not presented that way. Well, anyway, one time I went to the
newsstand and saw one of those big, fat *Amazings*—I don't
remember the date—with a Burroughs story listed on the
cover. I picked it up for the Burroughs and made the fatal
mistake of reading the rest of the magazine. I remember that
issue had an Eando Binder story, "Adam Link Saves the
World," I think, and a great short novel by Edmond Hamilton
called "Treasure on Thunder Moon"—I thought it was the
finest piece of literature I'd ever read. I was just completely
hooked. And I really did the kind of junk I described in the
letters, hopping on my bicycle and barrelling back to the
newsstand and buying everything that had anything to do
with SF. It really happened—every month!

So, there I was in Cincinnati. During the war my father (the doctor) enlisted; they sent him to Crystal City, Texas
as the Medical Officer in charge of what they called an alien
detention camp—an internment camp for Japanese and Ger-
mans. Needless to say, he took the family with him. When I
got to Texas it was the end of my sophomore year in high
school. About 1944, my father was transferred to Galveston,
Texas, at the Marine Hospital there. But I stayed in Crystal
City, renting a room, because every time I moved I became
ineligible to play football, and football was THE big thing in
my life in those days. I wasn't about to miss my senior year,
so I stayed by myself. Then, after I graduated in '45, I came
to the University. My family was still living in Galveston.
About my junior year in college my father went to work in
the Veterans Hospital at Kerrville—my mother is still there.
My father is dead.

I went through Plan II at U.T. and got my B.A. there.
My English prof my freshman year was Harry Ransom, a
marvelous teacher. I think, if I'm not mistaken, that I was
the only boy from my graduating class at Crystal City that

went on to the University of Texas. Everybody else went to Texas A&M University. I was the maverick of the group. Plan II, as you know, doesn't have a major; it's an honors program in the liberal arts. I got my M.A. here with a major in English and minor in anthropology. I wrote my thesis on science fiction under Harry Ransom. Then I went to UCLA and took my Ph.D. in anthropology.

HALL: Did you start as an anthropology major in the master's program? There were mentions of an anthropology major in some of the letters.

OLIVER: No, not really. The way it worked was: I'd always been interested in anthropology. I got interested in it from science fiction; as you probably know, a great deal of SF deals with what really is a conflict between cultures. I was always interested in that. When I got to the university my freshman year, I took a couple of courses in anthropology and I liked it a lot, but I wasn't really hooked on anything specific; and I didn't take any more anthropology classes until my senior year.

A number of people had told me there was a professor on the campus I really ought to take a course from before I left—McAllister—and so I did, not really to take anthropology, but to take McAllister. He was one of those fabulous teachers that one rarely encounters, and from that time on I was in anthropology. But I was so committed—for a variety of reasons—to the English program that I took my M.A. in English at the same time I was doing graduate work in anthropology, and I actually taught English here (U.T.) for a while, at Ransom's insistence. But I knew that wasn't what I wanted to do. I found myself, in my English classes, talking about the Cheyenne or Comanche, so I went to UCLA and took a Ph.D. in Anthropology under Walter Goldschmidt.

BOLDT: You had a radio program for a while, didn't you?

OLIVER: Yes, but that was later. It was after 1955 when I came back here to teach anthropology. I hadn't finished my Ph.D., but had everything done but the dissertation. It was sometime after that I got roped into doing that disc jockey thing on KHFI. I did it for a couple of years, as I recall, right up until I left to go back to the U. of California at Riverside to teach for a year. Apart from that there wasn't much of anything.

BOLDT: Did you ever work for the *American Statesman*?

OLIVER: No. I've written a couple of articles from time to time, but never actually worked for them. As far as other jobs were concerned, there was almost nothing. There was a period in Cincinnati, actually, where I worked for a record store, but that was a long time ago.

HALL: You started publishing as an undergraduate student. I have a letter from one of your roommates commenting on one of your stories that it was a great piece, etc., and that it's immaterial that Chad is standing behind me with a gun.

OLIVER: That's funny—I have no memory of it at all. Actually, I started long before that—writing, that is—even before I left Cincinnati. I conned my folks into buying me a used Remington and taught myself to type. This was when I was practically bedridden. I ground out all sorts of masterpieces, and sent them in to a variety of editors. I'll never forget how kind most of them were, considering the quality of what I was probably sending—they must have been pretty terrible. Almost from the very beginning—I must have been about fourteen when I began doing this—I hardly ever got a form rejection slip. They'd always write me letters, saying, "This shows a lot of promise. Keep trying" or "Do this, that, or the other." It was something that meant a great deal to me. I kept it up all the time I was in Crystal City, despite my addiction to football. I wrote all the time, not prodigiously, but always something, so when I finally did connect, it was not as if I had just sat down one day and tossed something off and somebody (Tony Boucher, actually) bought it.

To get back to your question, yes, I guess I was in college, because it was after I moved to Kerrville that I sold that first story. I'll never forget it. "The Boy Next Door" actually was a story I wrote for *Weird Tales*, and sent it to to them during the last years of *W.T.*'s existence when they weren't doing any creative editing at all. In fact, I never got any response from them—they just sent the ms. back in the mail. *The Magazine of Fantasy & Science Fiction* had just started up, and I'd read it and thought "here's a guy who'll probably appreciate my tremendous genius." And he did! I was just floored when I got the letter—I can almost remember it word-for-word. He was apologizing that he could only pay $100.00 for it and would that be satisfactory? Also, they were having some financial difficulty and he couldn't pay right away and I might have to wait a month or two. God—I'd have given them the story, I'd have paid *them*, to publish it.

BOLDT: The introduction to "Boy Next Door" mentions this was the first story you sold, but not the first actually published.

OLIVER: After Tony—actually McComas and Tony—bought the "Boy Next Door," I sold a story to *Super Science Stories*. The editor, if I'm not mistaken, was a man named Jakobsson, the same guy who later edited *Galaxy*. He bought a story called "The Land of Lost Content" that was published before the *F&SF* piece, but was written afterward.

HALL: Have you read much in recent SF literature and do you have any opinion on it?

OLIVER: I don't read science fiction, *any* kind of fiction, as much as I used to, because I don't have the time. It isn't that I've lost interest, it's just that I have to be fairly selective; therefore, I don't feel as familiar with current SF as I ought to be to make some halfway sane comment, and I certainly don't want to run down any writer with whom I'm not familiar.

On the other hand, I've read stories by Harlan Ellison, Spinrad, Delany, Aldiss, and Zelazny which I like. I was amazed when Harlan Ellison asked me for a story for *Again, Dangerous Visions*. (A lot of my early stuff, including *Shadows in the Sun*, was very non-traditional for the 1950s.) I guess that the most honest thing I can say about current SF is that I've read some stories that I admire very much, but much of it is just not on my wavelength. I think you could be corny and say that Mr. Gernsback's mansion has many rooms. You can't be static, you can't stand still. I don't care how traditionalist you may think you are, none of us wants to go back and write like Ray Cummings or Otis Adelbert Kline or even Edgar Rice Burroughs, for that matter. It's really a question of what direction the field will move toward, and how much of what's accumulated will be thrown away.

I don't know if this makes any sense or not, but I come from a school of different terms. I think literature took a wrong turn with James Joyce. Not that I don't admire *Ulysses*: it's a fascinating book, but I think it did more harm than good in the long run. I have always liked Joseph Conrad, and the early Hemingway tales like *The Sun Also Rises* and "Big Two-Hearted River," partly because I like trout fishing. And Steinbeck, despite all the criticism that's been levelled at him. In other words, I like a more traditionally-based novel, and, I fear, I'm reactionary enough to prefer stories with a beginning, middle, and end. I remember I took an English course many years ago in which the textbook was something called *Tradition and Direction in the Modern Short Story*, and they began with four short stories, traditional stories, as examples of what not to do. I liked all four of them better than anything else in the book. Given my druthers, I'll still read Poul Anderson.

BOLDT: Your first book was *The Mists of Dawn*; was the book written to order, or were you deliberately trying to penetrate the juvenile market?

OLIVER: *Mists of Dawn* was written shortly after I signed with my first agent, Scott Meredith. Meredith had a contract with the John C. Winston Company for a series of teenage SF novels, and he asked me to write one. I submitted an outline and a sample chapter, and that's how the thing began.

HALL: The reviewers tended to criticize this particular book because of your characterization of Neanderthal man as a nasty kind of ogre. Why did you focus on this particular culture?

OLIVER: To be honest, it was such a long time ago that I can't recall whether the topic was assigned to me or whether I just picked it at random. As far as the critics are concerned, you can respond by saying that no one can prove that he wasn't, either. Who knows? It's really not a factual error, or at least one I consider factual. It's a matter of taste or interpretation, and I think it's very definitely tied to a number of other currents. There really aren't any "fashionable" villains. You can't even make an Indian a villain. There has been a lot of discussion in recent anthropological literature to the effect that the conflict, if there was one, between homo sapiens and Neanderthal man took some different form. You see, at the time I wrote this book they were classed somewhat differently than they are now.

Now they're both placed in genus *Homo*, which just makes them different subspecies. But in the 1950s, they were considered a distinct species, and there was a general feeling of long-term conflict between sapiens and Neanderthal, a struggle obviously by our species. But apparently it wasn't that way at all. It was more a problem of occupying the same ecological niche, with one being more efficient than the other. But, if you go back and read the book, which I confess I haven't done in years, I dimly recall including some rather sympathetic passages about the Neanderthals, too, including one that had something to do with a Neanderthal child. You've also got to remember that the protagonist in this book is a young kid who suddenly finds himself going back in time. Chances are that if suddenly Joe Neanderthal came walking through the door now, we would regard him with at least some trepidation. So, I wouldn't necessarily object to this kind of criticism. It's not nearly as annoying as the comments of Kingsley Amis, who criticized *Shadows in the Sun* because, he said, the protagonist was utterly unbelievable, a 6'3" anthropologist who lived in Texas. I was guilty, as authors often are, of writing about myself, and while I may be lots of things, I'm not unbelievable.

HALL: Many things in your books appear autobiographical, that being one.

OLIVER: *Shadows in the Sun?* I don't think the character is particularly autobiographical, except that if you happen to be a big man, as I am, it's easier to write about a big man, since that's what you've been all your life. He also smokes a pipe and things of this kind.

HALL: This gets into the area of reading into a book things that weren't put there by the author on a conscious level.

OLIVER: You never know. We talked about "The Boy Next Door"; I don't know if you remember the story, but in effect, it's modeled on an experience I had as a child. There was a radio program in Cincinnati where, if you accumulated enough coupons, you could go down and be interviewed on the air, and I was so turned off by all these saccharin interviews—"What have you been doing all weekend?" "Oh, I've been playing with my dog..."—that I thought it would be fun to have a character who would say, "Wow! I've been killing people!" Anyway, the character was named Jimmy Walls and Jim Walls is my oldest friend. He and I went through high school together and he still lives here in Austin—he runs The Pier on the lake, a classy beer joint.

Anyway, his mother got hold of that story. She interpreted it to mean that I was literally saying that Jimmy Walls went out and killed people, and she went around to all the newsstands buying copies and burning them. She took it dead seriously. And so have a number of critics, talking about the profound point I was trying to make about the nature of society. I was just having fun.

There is probably more that is autobiographical in *Shadows of the Sun* than in anything else. After all, it is about Crystal City, and I was there...

BOLDT: It fits, except for the geographical location.

OLIVER: Did I move it?

BOLDT: You ran it 180 degrees in the opposite direction, out in the West where there's nothing, not even a highway, present.

OLIVER: That was clever. I did the same thing in *The Shores of Another Sea.* Actually I located it correctly, but I changed place names around so that if you actually went to whatever I called it in the book, you wouldn't find it there. Mitaboni, I think I said it was in, and Mitaboni is clean in the other end of Ukambani. I don't know why I did it. I guess it's a device intended to say, "Look, this is based on a real place, but I don't really mean that one." There are a few changes.

There weren't any aliens in Crystal City, except me. I was the alien Yankee.

HALL: Out of curiosity, "Pilgrimage" is apparently one of your favorite stories, according to comments I've seen elsewhere.

OLIVER: Actually, no, not that I don't like the story, but I'm somewhat ashamed of having written it. "Pilgrimage" is about my wife's home town, Jefferson, and the image that comes through—satire, irony, whatever you want to call it—represents a point of view that I don't hold any longer; it some caused unhappiness to people in Jefferson who read that story. I guess that is an age-old problem for a writer. But these are people whom I like, people that I would not willingly have insulted for the world. Those people have always been very kind to me, so I do have this ambivalent feeling toward it. I like the story, but in a way I wish I'd never written it. I didn't mean it quite as harshly as it came out in print—again, I was just having fun, and there are some funny things which can be said about Jefferson. But as you get older and have children of your own, you get to the point where you catch yourself thinking, "If I had to pick a place where I'd want my kids to grow up, I could do a lot worse than Jefferson." And feel rather more comfortable with them growing up there than here in Austin.

You like different stories for different reasons. I suppose to some extent it depends on what day you catch a writer. There are ones that more or less stick in my mind, that I'm fond of for one reason or another. "Artifact," for example, a longish short story, and "Didn't He Ramble," the jazz story. I think "A Stick for Harry Eddington" is a good story, too, but it's very difficult to judge your own stuff.

You like to think you're getting better. I don't have as much time to write as I wish I did, and I haven't been very prolific since I've been fouled up with being chairman. But all that's going to end soon. I think I've learned a few things—I hope I have. Dick Matheson used to be terribly annoyed; the first story he ever wrote was "Born of Man and Woman," and apparently it's the only one anyone ever remembered. He's gotten to the point where he just hates it because the implication is that you haven't written a damned thing since that anyone can recall.

Of my novels, I liked *Unearthly Neighbors* least—that's not my title, by the way. I hate the title and maybe that's one thing that puts me off. I called it *Shoulder the Sky*, from Housman. It got changed because some guy had written a book about the Air Force that came out right about the same time with the same title. So Ballantine stuck *Unearthly Neighbors* on it, which I think is just ghastly.

If you'll notice, if my memory is not playing tricks on me, this is the only one of my SF novels not firmly rooted in the present. I'm not sure how much of this I've done as conscious policy or whether it's just worked out that way, but all the others are either set in the present or begin in the present, or they touch the present pretty closely, one way or another. I suspect that's another reason I'm less fond of it. It's harder for me to get a degree of reality into a story if I don't have a touchstone. I like science fiction that's not too far out, that has something that's recognizable not just to other people, but to me, so that the thing has meaning. I think that you could eliminate *Mists of Dawn* simply because it's a juvenile. I had some fun with that, by the way. There was a kind of formula you were supposed to use in writing for the whole series; every chapter, for example, was supposed to end with a shattering climax, to make Joe Blow, age fourteen, rip on through the novel. But I compromised, and—not consistently, but frequently—alternated chapters, with some which were all plot and others that were cliffhangers; in other words, one for me, and the next one is there for the story.

I think *Winds of Time* is a mixed bag, in that there are some things I like very much and other things I just don't care for. That leaves us with three. I guess I like *Shadows in the Sun*, but what I really mean is that it's somewhat closer to me than the others. I have not gone back and re-read it, and I'm sure if I did go back there would be lots of things I wouldn't care for. But I did like both *The Wolf Is My Brother* and *The Shores of Another Sea*. I worked a long time on the former book, particularly.

I started writing *The Wolf Is My Brother* before I left for Africa and I wrote a fair amount of it there in the evenings and sometimes when it was raining so hard I couldn't get out—you may remember from *The Shores of Another Sea*. I sometimes think my Comanches sound more like Kamba than anything else. I spent a good five years on that book, and I spent three years on *The Shores of Another Sea*. I don't mean constantly, but that's what I was working on. What finally came out is radically different from what I started with. It began life as a straight novel.

I never talk about things when I'm writing. I realize that this sounds terribly superior and smug and all that, but, in my experience, there are two kinds of writers—the talking writers and the writing writers. The guys who spend all their time talking about what they are going to do and what they're doing very seldom write anything. I find it very hard to talk about works in progress—the story just goes dead on me, because whatever it is that you're trying to get down on a piece of paper, that makes you want to write the thing in the first place, can be dissipated very easily. After all, that's what you are doing when you're writing the story. So I never talk about anything I'm writing, and actually very seldom about anything I've written, either, unless someone asks me, point blank. It's not that I'm secretive, but I have known writers—Chuck Beaumont was one—who were always full of what they were writing, right then, and had to talk about it, and couldn't wait to rip a page out of the typewriter and read it to you, whether the thing was finished or not. I've never been that way.

BOLDT: Your collaborations with Beaumont carry this tone.

OLIVER: We had more fun doing those stories than anything I've ever written. I have never really been able to collaborate with anybody else. There was a story that came out with my by-line and Garvin Berry's on it, you may have noticed, a very early story in *Super Science* called "The Blood Star"—not my title, either. He didn't write it. What happened is that we'd kicked it around for a long time, and part of the plot was his. I thought it was only fair to stick has name on it. Actually, Chuck's the only one I've collaborated with, and just on that one kind of story. We had a ball. Everything he wrote just knocked me out. We did it in sections. He would sit down and write a thousand words, then give it to me, and I'd read it and type the next 1000. He really broke me up—it was one of those happy things where we each amused the other. I remember taking his section of manuscript and reading it, and actually falling out of the chair, laughing, and then going down and trying to do likewise.

One of those stories that we wrote together was never published. I don't know what happened to it—it got lost somewhere when Chuck died. It was called "The Rest of Science Fiction." We took all the plots we hadn't been able to use in "The Last Word" and "I, Claude," and took care of the rest of them. I remember nothing about it, except that a lot of it was horror fiction. The protagonists were the beautiful scientist and his mad daughter—we thought that was a good switch. It was great fun. I miss Chuck terribly—he was a great guy who met a terrible death, one of those awful things where you talk about a man getting trapped in his own plot, rather a Lovecraftian sort of a notion. I can never remember the name of the disease, but Chuck is the same age as I am, and he just wasted away with premature aging and senility. I'll never forget the last time I saw Chuck before he died—his hair had turned snow white, his face was lined, his hands were palsied. He could feel it coming on. Toward the end he was just a vegetable, couldn't even say yes or no. It was a perfectly horrible kind of thing for this wonderfully talented guy. I could tell you lots of stories about Beaumont, but I guess that's not what you want. That wasn't his real name, either.

HALL: That seems to be fairly common.

OLIVER: But Chad Oliver's my real name. His real name was Charles Nutt, and he figured that was not an ideal name for a professional writer. It's very indicative of the kind of guy he was that he would pick a name like Beaumont. Even when he was desperately poor he was very flamboyant. He only had one decent suit of clothes to his name, but it had a flashy, red vest, and when he really got hungry, he'd go down—not to some hamburger joint—he'd pick out the finest restaurant in Los Angeles, demand to see the manager, and say "Sir, I am Charles Beaumont, struggling young writer. If you stake me to a meal, one day you'll be famous." He was never turned down, either.

BOLDT: Are there any other writers other than Beaumont and Bill Nolan with whom you became acquainted in California?

OLIVER: Yes, I knew Richard Matheson quite well. Dick and I had never met, and at the time we were both writing for *The Magazine of Fantasy & Science Fiction*, appearing side by side. As I said, I didn't know Dick and didn't know he never read SF. I read a story of his that really impressed me, and I thought, here's this guy right here in Los Angeles, I'll just call him up. I did and said "Hi, Dick, this is Chad Oliver." There was this long silence, and then the single word "who"? He'd never heard of me, didn't know who I was, and so I went over and explained who I was and we got to be very close friends. The only other ones I knew were Bradbury, whom I knew fairly well, although we certainly were never as close as Chuck and I and Bill, who were all struggling young writers. Bradbury had already arrived and tended to be rather paternal in his attitude toward the young upstarts. That's not really a fair statement—he's a very generous kind of guy. I knew van Vogt, and some of the old-timers like Ross Rocklynne and Stu Byrne. They were all over the place. Aside from those, actually the only other writers I knew well were Walt Miller and Randall Garrett, who once spent a year here. I've known others casually.

I'm a member of both SFWA and Western Writers of America, but generally I'm not an organization man. I don't join things, don't like meetings, and hate conventions. I'm one of these odd people who, when I get a few spare minutes, would rather be down on the stream, trout fishing.

HALL: Is the increasing academic interest in science fiction really good for the field?

OLIVER: I'm not sure what you mean "good for the field." What I really think is that it is inevitable. In lots of ways, if only on one elementary level, I've always felt, in my prejudiced manner, that for a fairly specialized, even coterie-type of writing, there is a lot better writing in SF than in any other comparable field, at least that I know about, and that's been true for many, many years. The utter contempt with which it was so long received by outside critics certainly hurt the many serious writers in the genre, whose books were either simply ignored or utterly condemned and torn apart by persons who had no knowledge about what they were castigating. There was a lot of writing during that period that was a damn sight better than anything else out there, and I think that's still true. There is a definite tendency in this culture toward a sort of masterpiece-of-the-week club. I've gotten to the point I never go see a film anymore when someone says "this will revolutionize motion pictures," or is "the greatest film of the last five years." The same way with mainstream novels—they become the darlings of the critics for six months or so, and then you never hear of them again. There were lots of things being done that should have received more attention than they got, but how much effect the new academic attention actually has on the writing of science fiction is something else. I think you could even say that maybe there was an advantage in writers writing science fiction because they loved it, and simply did the best job they could without worrying about what some critic was going to say. There's always the danger of beginning to cast one's writings for the critic—it's the worst mistake you can make.

HALL: Did you write much for the fanzines?

OLIVER: No. There were a few things and doubtless some I've forgotten. I wrote a piece on Ray Bradbury for the *Ray Bradbury Review*, a one-shot that Bill Nolan put out years ago. I was never involved with the fan magazines, except for publishing my own one-shot. Garvin Berry and I put out *The Moon Puddle*, just one issue, the title being a takeoff on *The Moon Pool*, by A. Merritt. We had a lot of fun with it, but we never really intended it to be a series. I think we only ran off fifty copies—it's a priceless collector's item. I don't even know where my copy is. We wrote the whole thing except for one article that David H. Keller submitted, during a period when he was sending everything to fanzines. I had an article in there about Edgar Rice Burroughs, and Garvin had a perfectly marvelous thing on Henry Kuttner in which he set out to try to track down every penname Henry Kuttner ever used, which was an olympian undertaking. I knew Kuttner in Los Angeles, also.

HALL: What about using a pseudonym yourself?

OLIVER: I don't think so, or if I ever did, I don't recall it. I never had any reason to—I'm not that prolific.

HALL: Was that the primary reason for a pseudonym in those days?

OLIVER: It just looked bad to have a contents page entirely written by one individual, although sometimes they did that, more or less as a gimmick—I remember Don Wilcox wrote a whole issue of *Amazing* one time. What usually happened was that editors would assign pennames to secondary stories by the same author in the same magazine issue, both to secondguess the argument that "he really can't be good if he writes that much," and secondly, because some writers used radically different writing styles and wanted to keep such stories separate. Kuttner, for example, wrote totally differently as Henry Kuttner and as Lewis Padgett, and for a long time nobody knew who Lewis Padgett was. And then he and his wife C. L. Moore collaborated on a number of things and used another name, Lawrence O'Donnell. Keith Hammond was another Kuttner name.

HALL: Some of these writers were unbelievably active.

OLIVER: The guy that amazes me is Poul Anderson. He is so prolific, and the quality is so high, and he has been doing it for so long. Amazing. There are lots of writers who have creative spurts and turn out a lot of really fine things in a fairly short time, and then more or less tail off and just dribble out a story now and then. Ted Sturgeon was like that; he wrote very little after a certain point. Heinlein was another who had a fantastically creative explosion early in his career, again under a variety of names. Here's a guy who contributed a tremendous amount to science fiction, particularly in terms of technique. During the early 1940s, when Heinlein was really turning stories out, both under his own name and as Anson McDonald, I think it would be very hard to point to any comparable three-year period in the history of SF in which so many new ideas were being generated by one person.

But someone who can sustain it over a long period like Poul has done is really amazing. I knew him, too, but not well—Poul lived in Berkeley. Several times when I went up to see Boucher I talked to Poul. I admire him very much. It's the kind of thing where there are not too many Poul Anderson stories you can look back on and say, "Boy that's the greatest thing I ever read," but on the other hand there are very few you'll put down and say, "Boy that's a total waste of time, a real stinker." He's a real pro.

HALL: Both of these men wrote primarily for *Analog*. What about you?

OLIVER: I guess I ought to set the stage and qualify a bit. I never met John Campbell. During the period I was writing a lot for

Astounding/Analog, under its various titles, John and I corresponded prodigiously, and I gather after the fact that this was more or less a requirement if you were going to write for Campbell, that you get involved in these endless arguments and discussions by mail. I don't know how he did it. He used to send me utterly fantastic letters—twenty-seven pages, single-spaced, of them. This was a busy man, you understand. John read virtually everything that came in himself, unless it was obviously illiterate. His assistant, Kay Tarrant, weeded out the stuff that was just hopeless, and he read everything else, and then wrote tremendously about it to his authors and prospective writers.

Let me say this: Campbell was probably the single most influential man in the development of what we call modern science fiction. This is beyond argument. If Campbell had not come along when he did and done what he did with *Astounding*, the whole course of science fiction would have been radically different. His influence was definitely beneficial. Apart from everything else, he was an amazingly creative editor, although not in the same sense that Tony Boucher was. Campbell's talent was not in taking a manuscript and saying, "this is what's wrong with it, do this that and the other, but do it your way"; instead, Campbell had the ability to find writers, stimulate them, and make them want to write for him, in his way. One way he did this is what's been called "education by irritation." Campbell had a habit of throwing out controversial statements and remarks, getting his authors so mad that they would promptly sit down at the typewriter and write a story to refute him—or agree with him. He got you involved. The result: just look at the writers this guy found. It's incredible! I respected and admired him a great deal. I suppose that ultimately it comes down to what you feel your view of science fiction is and how important you think it is. If you once grant the premise that it is worth something, there's nobody more responsible for what it is today than John Campbell.

On the other hand, the thing that always annoyed me about John, and it is something I found almost incomprehensible in a man who was a writer himself (and a rather good one too, not so much under his own name, but as Don A. Stuart), was his total lack of concern with writing *quality*. He didn't care, at least so far as I could determine. If he liked the idea, and if it was written just well enough to hold somebody's attention, that's all he demanded. I'm not so sure it was so much a hostility on John's part toward fancy writing—"trick writing," he often called it—he just didn't give a damn. If he got a story that was written in trick prose, and it happened to punch one of his buttons, and was comprehensible to his readers, he'd print it; but he just was not interested in writing as such, or literary quality, and this I found hard to take. It's one of the reasons for the curious status of *Analog* during the 1960s and '70s. Here was a magazine, that in its own way, was the best magazine in the field. It had a bigger circulation than any of its competitors, but when you picked it up, there wouldn't be a name on the contents page that you ever heard of before. None of the big names in science fiction wrote for *Analog* during this period, and it was supposedly the showcase of the field.

With regard to his editorials, that's a different can of worms. John was always, or liked to think of himself, as an iconoclast, an individual, idiosyncratic, always going against whatever the popular current might be. He had this image of himself. Nobody agreed with everything John Campbell said, including, I suspect, John himself. John was just one of those guys who automatically opposed the popular point of view, whatever it was, and was always trying to make an argument for the other side. I think a lot of what he said was highly dubious, the alleged racism, for example, and a number of other things. I also didn't share John's interest in Psi factors and all that stuff. We used to argue endlessly about this. I think John had a lot of peculiar ideas—about history, for example, and certainly about anthropology; but at the same time you've got to say that he was no fool. Other statements made a certain amount of sense, even if he did tend to push things further than most people would. He had a talent for not being impressed by a lot of fancy names, by footnotes and verbiage, and of going right to the heart of an argument and saying, "Hey, wait a minute, have you ever tried looking at it this way?" That's not a particularly popular thing to do, but maybe it needed doing.

Whether you agreed with him or not, you had to admit he made some valid points! What a terrible world this would be if things were completely non-controversial all the time. And God knows that Campbell's remarks were not nearly so controversial as the remarks made on the other side. It's also becoming rather more respectable—some of it. For a long time John questioned the idea that everything in human behavior was a matter of conditioning, or a matter of culture, a stock assumption of the social sciences for many years. Along come people like Robert Ardrey and Desmond Morris, and on a scientifically more respectable level, people like Konrad

Lorenz and Sherry Washburn, who are now saying exactly the same thing. John's arguments were never wholly nonsense.

HALL: We talked earlier about academic criticism of science fiction. But the first critics of the field were the writers themselves.

OLIVER: Yes, we never had a true critic of SF until Damon Knight came along, and I tended to disagree emphatically with much of what he said. He did some very worthwhile things—his essays on van Vogt, for example. The only trouble with Damon's criticism was that he didn't have the tact that Boucher had. He often destroyed a writer's work, and I suspect some of the authors he commented upon would just want to slink away in the night and never write another line. Tony had this marvelous facility, even if he didn't like a story, of making you want to continue; he also tried to help you, by providing some concrete suggestions for improvement.

HALL: Blish was another major early critic of the genre.

OLIVER: Blish was also a James Joyce scholar, among other things, another cerebral type who tended to question our origins: "Is this all that science fiction is?" You know, that kind of comment was levelled at SF for many years, mostly by people who didn't know what they were talking about. Of course, there's a small grain of truth in all such statements, that one of SF's major problems is its lack of characterization, that many of the stories contain no recognizable human beings. In fact, somebody once wryly commented that robots are the most human people in science fiction. On the other hand, many stories were so terribly intellectual and cerebral that they just never had any force or power—which seems to me the ideal fictional medium for somebody like James Blish or Damon Knight.

But you must realize that I'm quite unlike most SF writers that I know, for better or for worse, and I've worked largely isolated from the mainstream, or whatever you want to call it. Thus, my conception of what science fiction should or can be, and the kind of book I myself would like to write, is probably very different from what most of my contemporaries are or were trying to do. So I guess it's only natural that I like what I'm trying to do, although not saying I'm doing it correctly; and I've never read any criticism of SF that seemed to address itself to the same set of problems I would address if I were writing it—but then I'm not going to write criticism, so we'll leave it at that.

HALL: Have you done anything with your manuscripts, or made any similar provisions?

OLIVER: No. It was only a few years ago that suddenly the notion percolated that these things might have some value someday. I haven't kept a tremendous amount of materials from the early days. I've still got some boxes of stuff in Kerrville—I don't even know what's in them. The last time I looked there were some original manuscripts and working notes, and things like that, but for the last four or five years, I've kept everything in meticulous order, including working notes, first drafts, typescripts, notes for myself, and everything else, so I will have it in the future. For earlier years, I think I've got the original manuscripts of almost everything I've ever written, or at least a carbon of them. As to what I'll do with them ultimately, I really haven't thought about it. I've just now gotten to the point where I've stopped throwing things away. A lot depends on whether at some time a specific institution had an interest in my stuff, where it wouldn't just sit in a box somewhere, where it might prove useful.

BOLDT: Outside of your personal papers, what sort of SF library do you have?

OLIVER: I'm in the process of designing a study for myself. We've got fifteen acres out here, and a very small house. I originally had one room I could use as a study, but that was before my son came along. All I've got now is a desk in a bedroom, which is where I started out umpty-ump years ago, and we just don't have room to store much of my stuff. When I get the study built finally I can get everything together, and I'll bring it up from Kerrville. To answer your question, during the period when I was reading everything, I kept everything, from 1941 or '42 through the mid-1950s. I've got virtually everything—magazines, paperbacks, hardbacks. Prior to that, I have scattered stuff. I went back and bought a lot of early *Amazing*, *Wonder Stories*, *Weird Tales*, and so on, and I kept everything. I'd say the collection is probably very good up through 1955-1956, and very scattered since then. I just don't buy anything like the books and magazines I used to, but virtually everything I glom onto, I keep.

SOME SECOND THOUGHTS
by Chad Oliver

Frankly, it is a trifle eerie to read an interview with yourself that was taped nearly fifteen years ago. My first impulse was to go back and rewrite the whole thing. However, it seems to me that whatever value the remarks may have boils down to this: that is what I thought and said at one particular place at one specific time in my life. Therefore, my editing was minimal: I tried to fix the syntax just enough for coherence, I corrected some spelling disasters, and I deleted several sentences that I should have never spoken in the first place.

Otherwise, that's the way it was.

A few comments on the interview. There are a couple of items in the interview that I would like to clarify or amplify. Who knows: someone may actually read this sometime. Bear with me, please, and I'll take them in the order in which they were discussed.

Anyone interested in the influences Dr. McAllister and Dr. Ransom had on me might check out an article I wrote. It's called "Some Blues for a Trio," and you can find it in a book with the forbidding title, *Texas, Our Texas*, edited by Bryan A. Garner, and published by Eakin Press (Austin) in 1984. The other member of the trio was Dr. Clarence Ayres.

It was painful to read the reference to Jim Walls, whose name I used in my first story, "The Boy Next Door." (His name also pops up in other stories of mine, including *Shadows in the Sun*.) Jim died of lung cancer five years ago, and the hardest thing I have ever done was to give the eulogy at his funeral service. His widow (Jean) and I still get together on Thursday nights and drink a few in his memory. I feel like I lost my right arm.

Concerning *Shadows in the Sun*, I have reread it now and wrote an essay on it for the new edition published by George Zebrowski in his "Classics of Modern Science Fiction" series from Crown. I examine in some detail the extent to which the book is autobiographical. And, dammit, I did not change the geographical location of the town I called Jefferson Springs. It is described as being between San Antonio and Eagle Pass, and that's where it is.

Concerning *Unearthly Neighbors*, I've reread that one too and written some comments on it for the Crown edition, which came out in 1984. Rather to my surprise, it was a good deal better than my memory of it. Only the author's opinion, of course. I suppose that quite often what we remember is how tough a book was to write, rather than what was actually written. My daughter, Kim, was born while I was working on the novel, I was teaching classes at eight in the morning, and—well, you get the idea. All aboard for the romantic life of a writer...

Chuck Beaumont, bless him, died of Alzheimer's disease. It wasn't a famous illness then, and none of us had ever heard of it.

I note with some dismay that at the time of the interview my son was three-years-old and I was about to build a study for myself out on Empty Acres. Well, I still don't have a study—just the old desk in the bedroom. About eight of the acres have turned into a subdivision which we call ShadoWood on good days and headache the rest of the time. And my son, Glen, is just finishing his junior year of high school. He shows dangerous signs of writing and directing talent—may the Lord have mercy upon his soul.

My Life and Hard Times—Update. My apologies to James Thurber for this heading. I have been asked to ruminate a little about more or less current Oliver events, and at the risk of terminal boredom for the reader we're off.

Incredible as it may seem, particularly to me, I'm Chairman again, and have been for the past five years. There is no fixed term—or sentence—for a Chairman. A Chairman serves at the pleasure of the Dean, who in turn serves at the pleasure of the President. (There is, however, a mandatory performance review at the end of four years.) People sometimes wonder just what it is that a Chairman does. Chairmen wonder about that, too. Structurally, a Chairman is somewhere between a tribal chief and a mother hen. A Chairman (or Chairperson or a Chaircreature) is the head administrative officer for a department. The Chair, with the advice and consent of an Executive Committee or Budget Council, hires and fires, sets salaries, and determines overall policy for an academic department. The Chair handles all complaints from faculty, staff, and students. The Chair must have the wisdom of Solomon, the hide of a bull, and the endurance of a robot. The only good Chairman is a dead Chairman.

I have been fortunate enough to win a couple of undergraduate teaching awards in recent years, one a Presidential (UT, not US) award, the other the Harry Ransom Award for Teaching Excellence. It is pleasant and gratifying to be recognized in this way, but I was probably a better teacher twenty years ago. As is true of many other things, teaching gets harder as the years go by. The students are as bright as ever, but the stamina of the professor is notably less.

For me, the happiest thing that has happened in the last decade or so has been the appearance in Austin of a wonderful group of SF writers. They range from the ancient (Neal Barrett, who is only a year younger than yours truly) to the relatively young (like Bruce Sterling and Lew Shiner). There is no way that I can tell you what it has meant to me to have people like Howard Waldrop and Leigh Kennedy and Steve Utley and Lisa Tuttle around. They are gifts from the gods, that's all. I don't know whether there is a "Texas School" of SF writing or not. I do know that they are a warm and immensely talented bunch of human beings, and I have profited both personally and professionally from their presence. I hope they all win Nebulas and live forever. My only criticism is that Howard catches more fish than I do. Of course, he uses ugly chickens for bait.

I wrote a textbook (*The Discovery of Humanity: An Introduction to Anthropology*, Harper & Row, 1981) that came along about the same time as my blood pressure problems. The juxtaposition of the text and the blood pressure was not a coincidence. I originally signed with Dick Heffron of Lippincott, saying in all my innocence: "Okay, I'll write you a textbook, but its going to be my kind of textbook." All was euphoria for a while, then Lippincott was sold to Harper and Row. Suddenly, new editors, squadrons of them. They said: "Hey, why isn't this like all other textbooks?" We fought over every line; somebody had taught them that plain English was a disease. Well, a portion of what I wrote survived. The book is doing fairly well, but I've never used it myself.

What else? I'm a grandfather now, via my daughter rather than my son. At least, my son hasn't told me that I'm a grandfather.

My wife, Beje, raises Arabian horses. They live better than we do. Beje tells me she will divorce me if I don't resign the chairmanship soon. [Oliver did in fact relinquish the chairmanship shortly thereafter.]

She always was the sensible one in the family.

Never Write Without an Ending. No more predictions, sports fans. There are two novels in my head; the trick is to get them out. I have some other stories to write. They will be written when the right time comes.

My dream is early retirement. Three years to go. Maybe.

The best thing about my life in science fiction has just been being a part of it. I love the stuff, I love the writers, and I love the fans. I've even learned to enjoy the conventions, thanks to the good folks at AggieCon.

Beware. One of the first signs of senility is sentimentality.

I'll go home now and kick the cat.

—Chad Oliver
Austin, Texas
1985

ABOUT HAL W. HALL

Halbert Weldon Hall was born October 29, 1941 at Waco, Texas. After graduating with a degree in biology, he taught high school for several years, before returning to North Texas State University for his M.L.S. (1968). Since 1970 he has been a librarian at Texas A&M University. In 1971, he began editing and publishing his annual index to books reviews in fantastic literature, *SFBRI*, which has been cumulated into three large volumes by Gale Research Co. His second major work is the annual *Science Fiction and Fantasy Research Index* (also cumulated by Gale in 1985), the standard guide to secondary sources in fantastic literature. In addition to these ongoing publications, he has also edited the excellent *Science/Fiction Collections* (Haworth Press, 1983), and has compiled *Science Fiction Magazines: A Checklist*, the preliminary version of this bibliography, as well as numerous essays and reference articles for the standard academic and library journals. He is currently finishing a large bibliography on western writer Louis L'Amour for The Borgo Press.

INDEX

"Le Vent Souffle où il Veut," B38b
"Vento del Nord," B34e
Les Vents du Temps, A4h, A4hb
Veter Vremeni, A4f
Vultos Sobre o Sol, A2k
"What Is Science Fiction," C3
"When Fiction Turns to Fact: We Live Together, or Die," C4
"Win the World," B8b
"The Wind Blows Free," B38
The Winds of Time, A4
The Wolf Is My Brother, A7
Die Wolf Mein Bruder, A7e
The Work of Chad Oliver: An Annotated Bibliography & Guide, G78
"*The World of Man*," C5
"The Worlds of Chad Oliver: A Biographical Introduction," G23

www.ingramcontent.com/pod-product-compliance
Lightning Source LLC
Chambersburg PA
CBHW051931240626
47153CB00004B/1453